The Secret Bookstore

A Modern Fable

By Magnus Fox

ISBN: 978-0995290617

ILLUMINATION PUBLICATIONS, 2016

www.thesecretbookstorenovel.com

In the middle of the journey of our life I came to myself within a dark wood where the straight way was lost.

-Dante Alighieri

...the separation between past, present, and future is only an illusion, although a convincing one.

-Albert Einstein

In The Beginning

A clock, a mouse, the sun, an oak tree and a turkey vulture argue about the meaning of life.

"To tell time," says the clock.

"To grow," says the oak tree.

"Surviving," squeaks the mouse.

"Being a light," the sun proclaims.

There is a pause.

"To reveal truth," says the turkey vulture.

I appear with a gentle whisper. I am Love. For where there is Truth, I AM. I have no body, but the clock, mouse, sun, oak tree and turkey vulture feel me as a warm breeze.

"How do you reveal truth?" I ask the vulture.

"Through my flight," the vulture answers, spreading out his mighty wings. "That is why I fly. That is my purpose."

"A man has asked to know his purpose in life," I say to the vulture. "You will help him. Truth is the place to start his story."

The mouse twitches its nose and pipes up: "What about a lie? That's interesting too. Wasn't Lucifer a liar? Every story needs a devil. I could be an instigator."

"What about the absence of time?" the clock asks. "How could there be a story without time? Start the story with a clock. Listen."

The clock magnifies the sound of its ticking, the sound reverberating through the earth.

When the sun doesn't speak, I ask him if he feels he is needed in the story. The sun is silent for so long that the mouse squirms and its whiskers quiver.

"Am I not the centre of the universe?" the sun says, glowing as brightly as though it was midday in the desert. "I'll be there even if I am hidden by clouds or muted by sunglasses. I will mark each day. Without me there would be no shadows."

"And you?" I ask the oak tree.

"I am shelter. I am shade. And I know how to keep secrets," the oak tree says, stirring and rustling her leaves. "I murmur, but never reveal what anyone has told me. I can help the man on his journey."

My presence intensifies and sounds like rushing waters.

"This man is honestly full of lies," I say. "I've chosen this sad and lonely man."

"Are the chosen without suffering?" asks the oak. "I remember the pain of nails being hammered into my trunk."

"The chosen are filled with suffering," answers the vulture, flapping his wings. "But suffering is not wasted on them. They are purified in the fires of truth."

"Go," I say to the bird. "Find the man. Be fearless. Remember: I AM always with you."

The vulture flies up and soars over dark forests to lead the way.

Seven Turkey Vultures And A Mouse

Once upon a September morning, Magnus Fox exited his condo and saw seven turkey vultures roosting on the shiny paint of his new red Porsche. Magnus shouted and dropped his briefcase. The birds slowly stood and shifted, as if they were in no hurry. He was so near he could see their short hooked beaks and bald heads. Waving his arms, he ran out into the parking lot. The vultures unfurled their wings and then one by one they launched themselves upwards, their wings loudly beating through the air. They circled above, the black silhouettes of their bodies cutting through the pale blue of the predawn sky.

Magnus inspected the hood and roof of his car for scratches. With relief, he noted that there was no damage, although he wondered why they had been sitting there. He glanced around the parking lot at the other vehicles. None of them had birds sitting on them.

He shook his head, and reminded himself that there was a big project due at work today and he didn't have time to be distracted by anything, especially not wildlife appearing outside his condo. He was an accountant and preferred to be in the office by 6:30 AM, as he did his best work before nine. He liked the silence of the empty office before his co-workers arrived.

He retrieved his bulging briefcase from the building entranceway, and placed it in his passenger seat. The leather seat was cool as he slipped behind the wheel. He inhaled deeply to fully smell the scent of new car. It actually made him feel slightly nauseous, but as it represented a recently purchased vehicle, he felt pleasure upon noticing it.

Magnus sped out of the parking lot and down the quiet street to get away from the vultures as quickly as possible. The vultures made him think of his own death. This surprised him. He believed that he was a man of complete logic and reason. He was not superstitious. Besides, he was just thirty-three and death was far in the future. He hoped.

The vultures meant nothing, he reassured himself.

A few seconds from his condo, he glanced in his rear view mirror. The seven birds were flying along behind the vehicle, easily maintaining his pace. The skin at the back of his neck prickled.

He pressed down on the gas pedal and focused on the car. He felt more agile in the vehicle than he did in his own body, and enjoyed the feeling of speeding. Last week when he had gone to the car dealership, he'd planned to buy a fuel-efficient domestic car that would last him for years. The car salesman had convinced him that a Porsche would make him feel suave and athletic. Magnus felt neither of these things when not driving the Porsche, and had allowed himself to be talked into the purchase.

Now, as he leaned into a tight turn, he glimpsed something moving beside him. There was a plump grey mouse sitting on his passenger seat. Its whiskers quivered as it looked back at Magnus intently with beady black eyes. Magnus jerked in surprise and swerved out of his lane. Quickly, he spun the steering wheel and straightened the vehicle back to his own side of the road.

He stole another peek at the passenger seat. The mouse was still there, now cleaning its face and whiskers with its tiny paws. Magnus turned his attention back to the road and slowly removed his foot from the accelerator. Then he looked again. The mouse squeaked and then froze, staring back at him, its paws suspended in mid-air. Magnus looked back to the road ahead. A minute later, he took a deep breath and took another glance beside him.

The mouse was gone.

Magnus clenched his jaw as he visualized the rodent chewing at the wires under the dash, clawing at the rich leather of the seats and leaving droppings throughout his new car. He tried to pull his mind away from the mouse and to his work project, but kept imagining the tiny eyes watching him.

A few minutes later, when Magnus glanced in his rear view mirror, he saw the mouse sitting in the back window. It again squeaked when Magnus' eyes caught him, but it didn't move. A second and a half later, Magnus turned his attention back to the road.

The rear end of a garbage truck loomed before him. He slammed on the brakes.

He was too late.

Just before he crashed into the truck, his life failed to flash before his eyes. Instead rows of numbers raced towards him.

No, he thought in horror. *Has my whole life has been reduced to nothing but numbers?*

An Opportunity

Magnus stumbled through the narrow gap where the driver's door had been. It now decorated a hedge twenty feet away.

The garbage truck driver shook his head and looked at the totalled red Porsche. He said, "It's a miracle that you weren't killed."

Instead of answering, Magnus looked upwards. The garbage man followed Magnus' gaze. Seven vultures circled overhead.

"Disgusting birds. They'll pick your bones clean and leave them to bleach in the sun, if they get the chance," the driver said. "Man, you're lucky they're not eating you right now."

A lump formed in Magnus' throat, so he couldn't speak. He felt like vomiting as he realized how close to death he had come. However, he kept his face as composed as possible.

"You're too calm, mister," the garbage man said, clapping Magnus on his shoulder. "You must be in shock. Can you speak?"

Magnus shrugged. The man removed his hand.

Magnus felt an emotion bubbling inside of him that he could not describe. Perhaps the garbage man was right and he was in shock. However, he didn't feel upset about the car. He was shaken by the fact that instead of his life, he had seen numbers flying towards him at the moment of near-death. Also, he worried that he must have missed opportunities in his life to live his true purpose.

Last night, as he had been falling asleep, he had wondered what his true reason for existing might be. It distressed him to think that there was no more meaning to his life than being an accountant, earning, saving and spending money.

The garbage man punched his shoulder. He smelled like stale cigarettes. Magnus still felt sick and the smell repulsed him, so he moved away from the man and the scene of the wrecked car. He gulped several times, until the lump in his throat disappeared and he was certain that his face was perfectly composed. He had learned this trick as a young boy, when he discovered that there were many benefits to hiding all his feelings from both adults and other children.

Magnus ignored his nausea, wondering if he had tempted the fates to notice and punish him for buying the impractical Porsche. Instead he should have bought a practical car; then none of this would have happened. He turned his back on the tens of thousands of dollars of worthless scrap metal, the scene of his near-death, as the sound of police and ambulance sirens pierced the air.

He was not dead. He had survived. He still had an opportunity—for something.

But for what? he wondered.

The paramedics found not a scratch on Magnus Fox. Although they urged him to go to the hospital to be examined by a doctor, he insisted he felt fine, and refused.

Next he spoke to a police officer. When recounting the details of the accident to the police, Magnus didn't tell the officer about the mouse in his car. He wiped sweaty palms on his suit pants as he wondered if that was considered withholding evidence; he prided himself on being scrupulously honest.

"Are we done here?" Magnus asked the officer, as he handed over the last of the forms he had to fill in. "I don't want to be late for work."

"You're white as your shirt, sir," the officer said. "Why don't you take the day off?"

Magnus looked blankly at the officer. In his nine years at this current job, he had never missed a single day of work, not even the time he got pneumonia. They needed him at his company. If he hurried, he could go home, change into clean clothes, catch a taxi and be at the office before nine.

"I'll give you a ride home," the police officer said, shaking his head.

The Woman In Green

Magnus had the police officer drop him off a few blocks from his condo, wanting to walk a little to clear his thoughts before continuing on with his day.

He was surprised to feel a throbbing pain in his knee, since when the paramedics had examined him he'd felt nothing unusual. The knee-pain forced him to move slowly, so it seemed like he would never reach his home. He felt much older than thirty-three as he limped along, wondering what meaning his life had. Working fifteen hours a day, six days a week, couldn't be all there was to life.

He couldn't think of one person who would really miss him, if he'd died in the car crash. His parents had both died several years before. He had no siblings. No relatives lived nearby. He hadn't had a girlfriend in over two years, and he had little free time or energy to invest in a new romantic relationship anyway. His only friends were a few people from work with whom he sometimes socialized. He was an exemplary employee, and he was certain that he would be missed at his office—until they hired someone to replace him.

Sweat beaded on his face and trickled down his back. After wiping his forehead with a handkerchief, he paused at the edge of the river across from his condo. He counted a dozen vultures circling high above him, hardly more than moving specks peppering the clear sky. He again felt nauseous. He focused on the water to steady himself.

Immediately, he recognized this as a mistake. As he watched the grey water flow past, his stomach began to twist and turn. Goosebumps covered his skin. He'd never understood why, but he had been afraid of water and drowning for as long as he could remember. He took several steps back to lessen the risk of anyone knocking him in if they walked by, but continued to look at the water.

After Magnus had stared at the water for a few minutes, it no longer looked real. It looked *more* than real—like in a well-filmed movie where the scenery looked sharper and clearer and more beautiful than reality. It looked beautiful.

As he took a slow deep breath of the cool morning air, thankful to be alive, someone touched his elbow. He jerked and turned, startled to see a woman standing beside him. She wore a long green dress and had curly red hair. Her large green eyes and wide smile looked familiar, although he was certain he had never seen her before; it was as if he was remembering someone he had yet to meet, like remembering the future. She had a nametag pinned to her chest that announced her name was MATILDA.

"Do you want to walk on water?" the woman in green asked in a lyrical voice.

He blushed, and his hands grew clammy. They felt awkward dangling at his sides, and so he hid them away in his pockets. "No, of course not. I'm afraid of water. I can't swim."

"You want to walk on water," Matilda repeated.

This time it was a statement, not a question, he noted.

Matilda leaned forward and Magnus thought she was going to kiss his cheek. He leaned towards her in response. She was so close he could see her dark red lashes as she blinked. She smelled of lilacs and laundry that had been hung outside to dry on a sunny afternoon in the countryside. But instead of kissing him, she swayed back again. Magnus blushed at his foolish expectation. Embarrassed by his blushing, he blushed even more. He was relieved that she didn't comment on his red face. She turned and pointed at the water. He followed her gaze. The other side of the river was just visible through a swirling mist.

"I'm not the person you think I am," he said, looking behind him, suddenly thinking she must be speaking to someone else nearby. Beautiful women never just came up and spoke to him. But no one else was on the street.

"Wouldn't it be nice to show up to your own life?" Matilda asked.

Magnus nodded slowly, as his knee began throbbing

intensely. He loosened his tie and removed his suit jacket and hung it over his right arm.

This woman was different from any person he had ever met. He wanted to trust her completely, tell her what he was thinking. Even though he wasn't sure it was wise, the thought growing in him felt so intense that he blurted it out: "I don't want to be an accountant anymore. I hate my job."

He was shocked to hear his own words, but also relieved.

He pulled his tie off over his head. Then, as he dropped both it and his suit jacket to the ground, Matilda smiled at him with her eyes. They were the exact green of a polished fragment of glass he had once found in the school yard when he was a boy, and had pretended was an emerald. The kindness of her eyes gave him courage to believe that he might still have opportunities ahead of him. Perhaps thirty-three wasn't so very old. Maybe his life wasn't ending, but just beginning.

Then, with a shudder, he remembered his grandmother had repeatedly mentioned that Jesus was thirty-three when he was killed. Magnus' eyes flickered up to the sky, looking for vultures. A lone bird circled above.

"How far do you want to go?" Matilda asked, and gestured into the distance, across the river.

She rocked on her feet and then stood on her tiptoes, as if the earth would not contain her, and any moment she'd fly away. A breeze ruffled her wild hair. It looked like she hadn't brushed it for days and it was all the more beautiful to Magnus for being dishevelled.

When Magnus didn't answer, she asked: "One step, to prove you can? Or right across?"

"I need to go far away," he said, surprising himself again.

He could imagine himself walking away from his current life. He'd leave behind all his doubts and fears, and go towards something new and alive. He'd walk towards his purpose. He'd leave behind his old self.

Then he shook his head and rubbed a hand over his closely cut hair. The accident must have activated a long-unused part of his imagination, he decided. His own words and thoughts made no sense to him.

However, even though he told himself to hurry home to get changed for work, he didn't want to leave the presence of this mysterious woman. His feet felt like they were glued to the pavement. Returning to his normal life felt impossible.

"Do you want to see something miraculous?" Matilda asked.

Magnus cleared his throat and raised his eyebrows. "I don't believe in miracles. I'm an accountant."

"Sorry to hear it," she said.

Magnus rubbed his hands on his pants and stuttered, as he tried to think of something to say that might not make her sorry. He thought of several possibly interesting things about himself. He had collected stamps as a boy, and had found a rare stamp in his collection worth a thousand dollars. He could quickly multiply large sums of numbers in his mind. He knew the capital of every country in the world, and could list every country alphabetically. None of these seemed impressive enough to mention to a beautiful woman. In fact, they all sounded boring.

Then he remembered that he used to be able to do a handstand as a boy. He bent forward to try to do one right then and there. Even as he did so, he reminded himself that he had not attempted it for several years, and was afraid of embarrassing himself by falling. He stood up straight again.

"I'm sorry too," Magnus said.

"You want to step away from all doubt," said Matilda

She looked across the river so intently that Magnus wondered if she was seeing across to the other side or visualizing herself walking across the water's calm surface. Magnus imagined himself stepping out onto the water, holding her hand and walking over it beside her. He almost smiled at the image.

"Is it possible?" he asked.

As he gazed with her across the river, his heart pounded at this radical idea. He felt like she was tempting him away from his safe life for something dangerous, something laced with freedom.

Freedom…

This idea seemed just as likely to be poisonous as it might be the elixir of life. He wondered if freedom would bring him life. Or death.

She was so beautiful and charming that Magnus would have believed anything she told him. He didn't care how uncharacteristic it was of him to quickly trust a stranger with peculiar ideas.

"You want to do something impossible," she said. "You don't want to do it because it's possible."

As Magnus pondered her words, she tilted her head to the side. She wore three necklaces of polished green glass beads that swayed and tinkled against each other when she moved. The beads were the exact colour of her eyes.

"Could I really walk across it?" he asked, as the sound of the tinkling beads continued to echo in his ears.

"Anything is possible," Matilda said. She rocked again on her feet, standing on her tiptoes. "Of course, it's not probable."

Magnus' shoulders drooped in disappointment. He bent and picked up his suit jacket and tie.

"But once, you *knew* how to walk on water," she said. She continued to rock on her feet as she spoke. "We all did. It's just a matter of remembering. You just have to move forward step by step, as if you're a child with limitless belief. You just have to forget everything you've heard for years, telling you what you can't do."

Even though he didn't understand a thing she was saying, he wished she would keep speaking because he loved the hypnotic musical sing-song of her voice. Indeed, he loved everything about her—even the fact that her bottom front teeth were slightly crooked charmed him.

She moved her lips as though to speak, and he leaned in to listen closely. But then, instead of speaking, she pulled a business card out of her green sequined purse and handed it to him. The card smelled like dried leaves and pine needles.

"To help you remember," she said.

Magnus read the handwritten black lettering on the plain white card: *The Secret Bookstore*. The back of the card was blank.

"No address or phone number?" he asked.

"Then it wouldn't be very secret, would it?" she said, and her eyes closed as she laughed.

He laughed with her, at himself. Warmth spread from his heart through his chest and flowed down his arms and legs and into his hands and feet and fingers and toes. His entire body tingled with life.

"At the bookstore you'll find a book that teaches you how to walk on water," she promised.

Suddenly, fear crept into Magnus. He stopped laughing. "If I'm not an accountant, then what will I do?"

She fell silent too, and stopped rocking. With her slender hand, she pushed back a tendril of red hair that had fallen in her eyes. The glass beads tinkled again.

"The book will help you discover your life purpose. Find the store," she said.

"Will you—will you show me the way?" Magnus asked. He added in a small voice: "Please."

"I don't tell anyone how to get there. They need to find their own way."

Magnus turned from Matilda and stared out over the river. He wanted to prove himself to this beautiful woman. If she thought it was possible to walk across the water, it had to be true.

"Why do I need a book to teach me my purpose?" Magnus asked, looking back at her. "Why couldn't I just go out and walk across the river right now?"

She smiled and swept out a slender arm as though to say, *Go ahead and try.*

Magnus marched with determination up to the water. He'd go to the other side, and leave the smallness of the cityscape, his tiny, familiar, mundane world, and go towards a new purpose. His heart raced at the thought of freedom. He almost felt giddy.

But the water smelled musty, and a little like rotten fish. At the edge, he hesitated as he doubted himself again. His body broke into a cold sweat and his hands trembled as his old fear of water intensified. He clenched his jaw and forced himself to raise his foot towards the water. Then he jerked back from the river.

He blushed, ashamed that he had not been able to prove his bravery to Matilda. As he wiped sweat from his forehead, he turned to speak to her.

She had disappeared.

A Rare Moment Of Internal Honesty

Magnus' heart seemed to stop. Then the blood roared in his ears and his chest pounded. The most beautiful woman in the world had slipped away from him.

He looked up. The sky was empty. Not one vulture flew overhead. He felt utterly alone in the world.

He squeezed his eyes shut. The echo of their shared laughter came back to him. That moment with her had been one of the best of his entire life.

His eyes popped opened as he realized he was in love with her.

He wanted to dance right there in the street. He expected to hear a choir of angels. He glanced around, worried that someone might be watching him beaming like a fool or somehow listening in on his crazy thoughts. He didn't ever dance, especially not in public. He was surprised that logic and reason had completely abandoned him. Or, more accurately, he realized, that he had abandoned them.

Then he sternly asked himself what he was thinking. He deliberately pulled his mind back to his present life, thinking he could still hurry home, change and get to work on time. In response, his heart laughed at him and said he would look for the woman in green. The warmth he had felt when he laughed with Matilda again flowed through his body. His legs and arms felt energized, like they would start dancing, whether or not he gave them permission.

Magnus stood still, debating with himself.

He could search for the mystery woman.

Or he could go to work.

His mind, normally sharp and capable of quick problem-solving, had no ready answer for him. He thought that the warmth that had spread through his body must have seeped into his mind and rendered him temporarily stupid. Perhaps he had injured his head in the car accident, he worried, rubbing his forehead.

Coward, hissed a low gruff voice from behind him.

A sharp pain shot through his knee and he stumbled. He turned around to look for the source, but he only saw a crumpled paper cup and a seagull pecking at an empty chip bag. His eyes darted around, looking for the person who had spoken.

"Did I hear that?" he asked himself.

The bird squawked, as though in response.

"I must be imagining things. And I don't know why I'm

talking to you," Magnus said to the seagull.

He touched his heart with his finger-tips and then let his hand drop to his side.

In a rare moment of internal honesty, Magnus realized he didn't care what was brave or wise or what anyone would think; he would search for Matilda. His heart leapt within him, as he limped along the edge of the waterfront, looking for her in the entrances of nearby shops and restaurants.

Once he accidently stepped into a puddle of water. He glared down at his feet, wondering how he would ever walk across a river if he couldn't even walk across a puddle.

As he sought the woman in green, he realized with despair that he had already forgotten some of the details of Matilda's face. He knew her green eyes were round, but he couldn't quite remember how far apart they were. It was impossible to remember the exact shape of her upper lip. He touched his own earlobe, as he tried to recollect the curve of her delicate ear peeking through her wild red hair.

Again, he wondered why such a beautiful woman had had any interest in speaking to him. Each time he doubted that she had spoken to him, he clutched the business card and sniffed it to smell the scent of pine and dried leaves, as tangible proof of her existence.

Although he disliked talking to strangers, he asked the few pedestrians he met if they had seen her. Nobody had. Gradually the streets filled with people and vehicles. After searching for two hours, he finally stopped.

Magnus lifted his face to the sun to feel its warmth on his skin.

Above him three vultures circled. None of them flapped their wings. Riding air currents, they glided casually, almost leisurely. Magnus felt their eyes on him, like they were sizing up how much meat they would get from his carcass once he died. He shuddered, dropped his head and stared down at the business card in his hand.

The day had hardly begun. He was just thirty-three. Surely, it could not be his destiny to die today, not before he found his purpose in life. Not now, not when he had just met a beautiful woman he loved.

With a fingertip he tapped each letter of the business card, spelling out the words: *The Secret Bookstore.*

Hardly daring to hope, he whispered to himself: "Could there really be such a place?"

At The Office

In his office, just hours after the car accident, Magnus could not get the numbers to obey him. As he worked at his computer, plugging numbers into formulas and manipulating spreadsheets, they refused to do what he requested of them. This was unheard of.

He kept stopping in the middle of calculations to open his desk drawer to see if the business card Matilda had given him was still there. Each time, he was relieved to see it, and to know that he had not imagined her. And each time he looked at it, he felt unsettled, like he should be looking for the bookstore, not sitting here in his office.

At the waterfront, after not being able to find Matilda, he had decided to come into work. He had not known what else to do with himself. But since he had said aloud to Matilda that he hated his job, he could not hide this knowledge from himself any longer. He shifted uneasily in his office chair, not wanting to be here. However, a voice inside him, sounding suspiciously like his father, kept telling him that he was good at his job, so this must be his purpose. Another voice, the one that had looked with such horror at the numbers rushing towards him just before he crashed his car, kept saying: *There's more.*

But more of what? Magnus wondered.

He shook his head to stop his endless circling thoughts. He rubbed his swollen knee, and looked up at the window beside his desk to see if there was a turkey vulture outside. He looked at cardboard. He had forgotten it was there. Overnight someone had covered Magnus' office windows with pieces of grey cardboard. A co-worker had explained that the mini-blinds had been removed, and the new mini-blinds would come in tomorrow.

Magnus thought with irritation that even in prison there must be glimpses of the sky from cell windows. Here there was just the glow of computer monitors, cell phones and fluorescent lights. He missed the warmth of the sun on his face, heat that he had felt at the waterfront that morning.

He sighed as, again, he pulled out the card and smelled the scent of pine needles and dried leaves. Then he sniffed the stale and musty office air. As he placed the card back in his desk and closed the drawer, he heard an insistent tapping at the window. A turkey vulture, he thought, leaping from his desk to the window, ignoring the pain shooting through his knee.

He slowly pulled away the cardboard. A cardinal sat on the window ledge, pecking furiously at its reflection on the glass.

When it saw Magnus, it flew away. It left behind a small red feather stuck to the window.

Silly bird, Magnus thought. *Fighting with itself. No one is going to win.*

Magnus looked out and in the distance saw a lone vulture circling above a church in the east. The street below was busy with pedestrians scurrying to and fro. None of them were looking up at the vulture. He searched the street for a glimpse of red hair. After looking for several minutes and not seeing Matilda, he shuffled back to his desk, determined to lose himself in the stream of numbers. Being busy had always worked like an anesthetic for him. But instead of focusing on the numbers on the computer screen, he heard the echo of Matilda's tinkling necklaces and her laughter. As he remembered how he had laughed with her, he smiled.

Then, right there in the office at his desk, he laughed aloud to himself!

Immediately, he clasped a hand to his mouth and was silent. He raised his head and furtively glanced out of his office door. No one had noticed. Outside, in the open workroom filled with cubicles occupied by junior accountants and administrative assistants, heads remained bent over papers or phones or leaning towards computer monitors. There was the steady sound of the click of keyboards and calculators, and the low murmur of voices. He plastered a blank look on his face and bent his head over the file on which he was working.

Magnus thought of life as a long poker game; the secret to winning was keeping the perfect poker face. If no one ever saw what he was thinking or feeling, he never gave away his hand.

As a boy, he had discovered that enjoying complex math problems and reading books was a road to unpopularity and being bullied. When he didn't react, the bullies stopped teasing. When he hid his love for math and reading and instead joined the boys in playing sports, he made a few friends. Magnus made it a habit to assimilate everywhere he went. He had become proud of being a stoic, steady as a rock.

Now he clutched his head. The appearance of the turkey vultures and the car accident had left him feeling completely unsettled. He couldn't understand why it was impossible to forget a woman he had met only briefly. He took a deep breath, determined to hide all these feelings from everyone in the office.

Suddenly, he saw something move on the newspaper on his desk. The letter "I" on the word "think" shifted. He worried that he was imagining things and had lost his mind, but then he saw a fruit fly walk from the letter "I" to the letter "K."

As Magnus peered curiously at the insect, his boss, Linda, walked into his office. Magnus swallowed a sigh upon seeing her. She looked nothing like Matilda. Linda's coloured black hair looked unnatural and made her face look sickly white in contrast. She was short and had sharp shoulders. Linda looked down at the newspaper, and with a quick movement she squashed the insect with her thumb.

"Stop," Magnus cried, and jumped up from his chair. It skated across the room and crashed into a bookcase filled with client binders.

In the workroom heads rose from computers and turned to stare at him. He flushed at his outburst. He tried to put on his expressionless face, but he couldn't force the red from his burning cheeks.

"Go home," Linda said. "You've been rattled by the car accident. Take a day off."

"I want to finish this project by tonight," Magnus said weakly.

"We'll manage without you." Linda set her mouth in a straight line. Her lips were so thin they were hardly visible.

He tried to say, *You will?* Instead Magnus opened and closed his mouth, no sound coming out. He had believed himself indispensable to the company.

Linda pointed at the dead fruit fly, as if that was evidence of his strangeness. Then she leaned forward so close to Magnus that he could smell the peppermint she was sucking on, and whispered: "A few minutes ago I heard you laughing to yourself."

Magnus could not argue with the truth, nor could he lie, so he agreed to leave early. It was just noon. He called a taxi to take him home. He tucked the card for *The Secret Bookstore* into his pocket, and then packed up his computer and briefcase.

Magnus left his normally immaculately ordered desk in a slight state of chaos, covered with several unfiled and finished reports and a disorganized scattering of loose papers. This small act of rebellion loosened the tightness in his chest.

Several co-workers snickered as he walked by them. Magnus thought that they were laughing at him, but when he looked at them, he saw that they were talking to each other.

He worried that they had heard him laughing to himself. Or perhaps they had heard Linda tell him to go home. Then he wondered if something was wrong with his new suit. Magnus tugged at the sleeve and asked himself if it was too tight. He had gained a little weight over the past year, but surely the salesman would not have sold him a suit that was too small. He had been fitted and had it tailored for him. When he first put it on, it had felt like a second skin.

Now he worried that perhaps he looked ridiculous. He had always prided himself on looking so normal. Even more normal than anyone else. So normal that he was boring. He had often told himself he would rather be boring than eccentric. No one liked an eccentric. But he had always worried that for all his façade of normalcy, deep down he was a very strange and unusual person.

The bizarre events of the morning seemed to have confirmed this.

Have You Had Enough?

Outside on the street, a warm breeze blew around bits of dried leaves, a tissue and several pages from a newspaper. The bright autumn sun assaulted Magnus' eyes. He put on his sunglasses as cars honked in the distance. A rusty truck rumbled past him, echoing the unusual irregular beat of his heart. He paused. It felt like he could literally feel his soul rattling in his chest cavity. Then he sniffed and smelled asphalt. To eradicate that smell, he held the fragrant business card to his nose, and breathed in the scent of pine needles and dried leaves once again.

His tie felt as tight as a hangman's noose, like it had when he was a boy and his mother had forced him to wear one for Christmas photos. He loosened it. As he yanked it off, he noticed a man in a dark grey suit standing near his office building. Around his neck was a sign. Magnus stepped closer to him to read it. He read: *I am a Mute Street Corner Preacher. The Best Preacher You'll Ever Meet!*

The preacher handed Magnus a scrap of paper. On the one

side it said: *You have enough.* The other side said: *Have you had enough?*

"Yes. No. I just need one more thing," Magnus said. "To find my purpose."

The preacher neither nodded nor shook his head. Instead he stared past Magnus at a group of people walking down the sidewalk. Magnus waited for some reaction from the man, but the preacher remained immobile.

The taxi arrived, and Magnus dropped the piece of paper the mute man had given him onto the sidewalk to swirl with the other trash.

He held out his tie to the driver and said, "Merry Christmas."

The taxi driver raised an eyebrow and asked Magnus where he wanted to go.

"The Secret Bookstore," Magnus said, as he got into the back seat.

"Address?"

"Unknown."

The Old Tattooed Man

Not knowing where else to go, Magnus had the taxi take him home. As he got out of the cab, he saw an elderly man in front of his condo. The thin man, who looked like he was in his mid-eighties, vigorously clipped away spider webs with gardening shears, as though the webs were made of iron. Magnus wondered why he didn't just sweep them away with a broom. Because the old man looked like a homeless person, Magnus approached him cautiously.

The stranger wore a ragged short-sleeved shirt and faded jeans. His white hair was pulled back in a ponytail, and he had a long beard that reached his chest. His arms were covered with tattoos of strange symbols that looked like hieroglyphics. His deeply creased face suggested that he had had a hard life, but his expression was tranquil; so even if the living had been difficult, it seemed that he had made peace with everything that had crossed his path.

"Truly, you have to be assertive with spider webs," the man

said, when Magnus reached the steps. "This lets the spiders know that you're serious and they're not long for this world."

With the clippers, he pointed at the card Magnus held in his hand. Magnus pulled it back, afraid the man was going to cut it in two, or, perhaps, stab him.

"Who are you?" Magnus asked. "The gardener?"

"Could be," the old man said.

Magnus shuffled uneasily and didn't answer, deciding the less said to this strange man the better. The singing of a nearby cicada pierced through the silence. A second cicada added its strident voice.

"I see you've found a card for The Secret Bookstore," the old man stated. "There are rumours that there's a secret bookstore in the forest I live in."

Magnus inhaled sharply.

"I'm the forest warden there," the stranger continued. "People often wander by my house looking for the store. I wonder if the bookstore you're looking for is in my forest."

"Is the owner a woman with red hair?" Magnus asked.

He straightened his back, and put his weight on his non-injured knee, as he wondered why this man from the forest was here in front of his building in the city. He tried to place the man's accent, but it was unrecognizable. It spoke of everywhere and nowhere.

"I've heard from wayfarers that you cannot buy a book there," the man said. "The owner gives you the book that you need. Truly, the only price is making the effort to find the store. And if you're not ready for a book, the owner won't give you one."

"I need a book explaining how to walk on water..." Magnus' voice trailed off.

As he heard himself speaking, he felt foolish. He dropped his eyes from the old man's wrinkled face to his shoes. Several hours ago, such a thought, such words, would never have come from him.

The man pointed up at the birds circling overhead and asked: "Are turkey vultures following you too?"

"Since the day began." Magnus wiped his clammy hands on his suit pants.

"Beautifully designed," the man said.

"They're ugly," Magnus said. "I hate their bald heads."

"They're bald so they don't get bacteria caught in the feathers there."

"I'd rather be followed by some other bird." Magnus shuddered.

The man clipped several more spider webs. A spider dangling from a thread scurried upwards and disappeared under the roof. Magnus empathized with the creature, as it felt like his own life, which he had so carefully built, was being shredded to pieces.

"See how they wobble slightly?" The old man pointed again with his shears. "That's how you know it's a turkey vulture flying overhead and not a hawk or eagle. As they catch the wind currents, they teeter. They've been following me for fifty years. I've outlived many turkey vultures. By constantly following me, they've compelled me forward. But you don't have to travel as much as I did. You don't even have to go to the bookstore to discover how to walk on water. This is all you need."

The man picked up a package that was lying near his feet and handed it to Magnus. The striped green and blue wrapping paper had bits of dried grass and flowers embedded in it. Magnus pulled off the wrapping to reveal a brown leather book.

"It's the less adventurous route, but safer," the man said.

Magnus glanced through the book. The thick, creamy pages were blank and unused, but the edges were grubby and the leather cover scuffed and dog-eared. Magnus could not see how a blank book would teach him how to walk on water or tell him what his purpose was.

"Observe the vultures and write down everything you notice about them," the man said. "They will teach you the meaning of life and your purpose. Everything they do speaks of truth."

Magnus frowned and dropped the book to his side.

"I am going to find this bookstore," he stated firmly, his voice louder than normal. "I'm not planning to sit around and keep a journal."

"Am I annoying you?"

"No."

"I *am* annoying you. Just a little. You don't feel it. Truly, soon enough you'll feel more than you knew possible."

Magnus remained silent. This had been one of his strengths as a child: never answering bullies or tormentors, so eventually they left him alone.

"Would you believe me if I said that you would see the meaning of life in birds, if they were eagles or hawks following you?" the old man said. "Are vultures not dignified or beautiful enough? Do you know vultures have a superior sense of smell and better eyesight than most other birds or humans?"

"Who said that I was looking for the meaning of life?" Magnus demanded.

"Aren't you?"

Magnus held out the book to the man to return it, but the old man ignored him. A vulture flew low, so they could see its underside and the shadow of the bird moved right over them. The flapping wings rustled the air around them. The cicadas were suddenly silent. Magnus nervously shifted from foot to foot. Magnus guessed the vulture was at least six feet across from wing tip to wing tip. Magnus tensed his body so he wouldn't visibly shudder.

"That book costs nothing. It will cost you everything if you look for the store," the old man said as he continued clipping the spider webs. His vertebrae and sharp shoulder blades were visible through the fabric of his shirt. Although he was thin, he did not look frail. He looked fit and strong as steel, without any excess fat, and as flexible as a young child.

The man must be lying. For the right price someone would sell him a book, Magnus figured, and then he considered how much he might be willing to pay.

"Things that cost nothing are priceless. Far beyond all your savings," the man interrupted his thoughts. "You'll have to be brave enough to leave your job, your condo, your cell phone and gadgets and everyone you know. You might spend your entire life looking and never find it. Writing in this book is the easier way."

"Do you think I'm a coward?" Magnus asked. "Maybe I don't care to do it the easy way."

"Can't say you look brave."

Magnus now definitely felt irritated by the man, but he kept his face blank.

"I'm going to find this store," he vowed, as much to himself as to the old man. "The woman who gave me the card didn't say anything about writing things in a journal."

"I forgot how stubborn the young can be," the old man said. "But I'm no fool. I can see that the easy way of remaining here and observing vultures is going to be too hard for you."

Exasperated with the entire conversation, Magnus opened the building door, planning to dump the leather book in the garbage once he got inside. However, before he could take a step, the old man grabbed his elbow. Magnus was surprised at the strength of the old man's grip. Ropy muscles in his forearm rippled. Although Magnus pulled his arm back, the man did not let go.

"Magnus Fox, wait," the man said with authority, clearly articulating each word. "I know you."

Magnus paused, surprised that the man knew his name.

"Don't you recognize me?" the old man asked.

Magnus searched inwardly, trying to recall the man's face.

"I'm Glenn the Magnificent."

"Pardon?"

"Well, most people just call me Glenn. So I suppose I'm not as magnificent as I hoped to be."

The old man let go of his arm.

"Pardon?" Magnus repeated.

He must have misheard. When he was a boy, Magnus had given himself the nickname "Glenn the Magnificent." He had daydreamed about being a world-famous magician. He had chosen the name "Glenn" because it was both his own middle name and the middle name of his grandfather, whom he had loved and admired. But he had never told anyone about this fantasy.

"Don't you recognize me? I'm you," Glenn said. "I'm your older self. I've come from the future to help you find your life's purpose."

A Cliché

Magnus stared at Glenn.

"You're crazy," he said, finally.

"I am?" Glenn stepped towards him.

"You've come from the future?"

"Yes."

Magnus moved away from Glenn as he squeezed the leather book in his hands and held it in front of him like a shield.

"Why can we learn from our past, but not our future?" Glenn asked, as though it was the most logical question in the world.

"It's impossible. There are rules in the universe."

Magnus backed away until he felt the brick building wall behind him. He struggled to keep his face expressionless like an expert poker player, so Glenn would not see his terror.

Quickly, he tried to determine if Glenn looked like him, but Magnus could not see any resemblance at all between himself and this old man. This man was an inch shorter, and thin and wiry. He could not imagine himself with long hair and a long beard or tattooed arms.

"All right. Prove you're me." Magnus narrowed his eyes and clenched his jaw, as he stepped forward to challenge Glenn, deciding he would not let an elderly man intimidate him.

"Ask me anything about yourself," Glenn said. He put the clippers down and leaned against the building. He crossed his arms over his chest. The end of his long beard rested on his arms.

"What were my parents' names?"

"Herb and Dolly."

"Who was my first girlfriend?"

"Do you mean the girl in grade eight you gave lilacs to at her locker? Or Stacy, the girl in university that you dated for a month?"

This correct answer surprised Magnus, but he managed to keep his face blank and asked: "What's the last book I read?"

"You haven't read a book for pleasure for many years. You're referring to an accounting manual for work. Myself, I wouldn't call it a book. You don't remember the last real book you read."

During the exchange, Glenn remained perfectly immobile, but his eyes were locked on Magnus, like he was looking straight into his thoughts and even beyond that into his soul. Magnus paused to think of an impossibly difficult question.

"What name did I give to my blankie when I was three?" Magnus asked at last. He had never told anyone this. He stared back as intensely as possible at Glenn, determined to show he was fearless and would not be tricked.

"Benji. And no one else knows that you named it and thought of it as a pet animal. And the person you love more than anyone in the world is a woman named Matilda, who wore a green dress at the waterfront."

Magnus tried, but couldn't speak because of his dry mouth. His right eye twitched, as it sometimes did when he was nervous. Sweat beaded on his forehead. The pain in his knee was so intense that it felt like his leg might collapse under him. He leaned against the wall for support. Then he shuffled sideways, looking for the door with his clammy hands behind him. During this brief exchange, the cicadas had begun their abrasive singing again. Their sound came from various directions around them, so it seemed they had been surrounded.

"How—?" Magnus whispered.

"I was sent to help you find the bookstore."

"By whom?" Magnus felt the door handle and wrapped a hand around it.

"Would you believe it was for the sake of love?" Glenn said.

Magnus snorted.

"Oh yes, I forgot that I was once like you, the wise man of

reason," Glenn said, with a laugh.

Glenn's clear blue eyes were so calm yet so penetrating, that they made Magnus shiver. If Glenn noticed him trying to sneak away, he did not show it and continued to remain perfectly motionless, his arms crossed in front of him.

"Are you— God?" Magnus asked. He glanced up at a lone vulture circling above. Perhaps his last day on earth had indeed arrived. The God he had been raised on was old and wrinkled, with a long beard, like Glenn's. But he was never depicted with tattoos or as thin and disheveled, like a homeless man.

Glenn's lips turned up at the corners in a boyish smirk. In spite of his advanced years, he looked youthful. As Magnus sensed that the man was mocking him, his fear disappeared. This old man had to be playing an elaborate trick on him. Perhaps some co-workers or a neighbour in the condo had put him up to this gag. They had researched Magnus and told this man everything about him.

"I refuse to let you remain a cliché." Glenn stroked his beard and then tugged the end of it.

"Pardon?" Magnus asked.

"When is a man in an eight-thousand-dollar suit not a cliché?"

Magnus stiffened. Glenn was right. He had bought the suit two days ago for exactly that price. It was meant to go with his new car.

He rubbed his forehead. He felt like he had hundreds of

scattered words trapped his mind, and as they darted around his head ached.

"Who are you really?" Magnus asked again, baffled at this man and the entire morning.

Glenn let go of his beard and continued to stare at him as though to challenge him. Magnus then noticed that Glenn's blue eyes were the same shape and colour as his own.

Magnus had never liked looking at himself in a mirror, although he never knew why it made him feel so uncomfortable. Now studying Glenn's eyes, looking for some resemblance to himself, he felt apprehensive, even though Glenn's eyes were gentle and patient and the skin at the corners creased with laugh lines.

Magnus turned away from Glenn to enter the building. Just as he grabbed the door handle, a butterfly with brusquely beating wings, noisy as a bird, flew towards Magnus, as though to attack him. Magnus swatted it away and ducked his head.

"Wrestling with a butterfly," Glenn said, with a chuckle. "And the butterfly wins. Don't fight so much. Lean into life. That's the only way to find the bookstore."

Magnus ducked again, and tried to jump away from the butterfly. As he did so, his injured knee gave out and he tripped over the threshold, falling and tearing the elbow of his suit. He allowed Glenn to help him stand.

"Now you have a hole in your fancy suit," Glenn said. "And you're thinking that this is the oddest, but most interesting day of your entire life. And you want to believe that The Secret Bookstore exists. And you're thrilled to be in love with a beautiful woman. Now you're not a cliché."

"Where is this store? Is it really in the forest where you live?" Magnus asked, feeling both hope and skepticism.

"Trust me," Glenn said. "Truly, it will take just fifteen minutes for me to show you the way to the forest."

"But how long does it take to get there?"

"Depends on how fast we walk. And if there's rain. And how many distractions," Glenn said. He pointed at the single vulture circling above them. "But then, consider the turkey vulture. Does it ever reach its destination?"

Magnus considered all this—an adventure with no time frame, no promise of success, no fixed destination.

"You're hesitating because you plan all your spontaneous actions," Glenn said.

"That's impossible."

"It's what you do. Last weekend you planned to spontaneously wander by a baseball stadium and see if you could buy a ticket off a scalper. You planned this spontaneous action two days before the event."

Partly to prove he could be spontaneous, partly because he didn't know how else to find the bookstore, partly to prove to himself he was brave, partly because he wanted to walk on water and taste freedom, partly because he didn't ever want to return to his office and didn't know where else to go or what else to do with himself, but mostly because he felt like a desperate man, Magnus agreed to go with Glenn.

The Meaning Of Life

Magnus left his computer and briefcase in his condo. As he stepped out of his bedroom, he realized that he had forgotten his cell phone at work. He paused and considered whether he should return to get it before going with Glenn. Then he shrugged and told himself going with no cell phone would be part of the adventure, and returned to the condo entrance. Glenn waited there, leaning on a carved wooden cane. Around his waist Glenn had tied a brown jacket with several bulging pockets. He carried an empty-looking canvas sack on his back.

They both limped down the sidewalk. Magnus wondered if Glenn was imitating his own limp and, without staring, tried to study how the old man walked.

"Yes, there are unavoidable similarities that we share," Glenn said, as he stroked his beard.

"Does your knee hurt?" Magnus asked, hesitantly, unsure if he wanted to find out that his knee would continue to bother him for the next fifty years.

"Not a bit," Glenn said. "I wouldn't stand for that."

Then Glenn laughed, so Magnus was unsure if he was being serious.

Magnus lived away from the downtown core in a quiet neighbourhood at the city's edge. Along the river were several low-rise, high-cost condominium buildings. Newly renovated brick houses with carefully manicured gardens and lawns lined the side streets. They turned down one of these streets now.

"This is all the meaning of life," Glenn said, gesturing down the street with his cane.

Magnus looked around and saw nothing significant.

"Look closely," Glenn said.

Magnus squinted and peered around him more intently.

"There's a man painting shutters," Glenn said. "There is someone mowing their lawn. Smell the freshly cut grass. Someone else is removing shingles from their roof. Look. There's an old man sprinting past that young lady who is jogging and out of breath."

"So? What should I be noticing?"

"And look there," Glenn continued. "A mother is pushing a child in a stroller. There's a woman wearing a kerchief on her head throwing bread crumbs to a fighting flock of sparrows."

"Yes?" Magnus asked.

"Living. That's it. That's the meaning. This *is* life."

Magnus wrinkled his brow. "I want to do something really significant. Something purposeful. Not mow the lawn or feed the birds."

After he spoke, Magnus' heart thumped loudly in his chest. He didn't know if it was because of his desire to find his purpose, or his fear of what was coming next.

"I spent three weeks carving this cane." Glenn stopped walking and tapped it on the ground. His beard billowed up with each tap. "I worked on it like I was making a gold crown for a king."

"Is that your purpose? Carving?"

"No, I'm here to bear witness, to make note of what I see. The most perfect day of my life was when I once watched an ant climb a tree, chased by its own shadow. I was there to bear witness. I had fulfilled my purpose for that moment."

Magnus didn't respond. Watching an ant seemed like an enormous waste of time to him, certainly not purposeful activity. He thought Glenn was either foolish or delusional or both.

"No one else can see what I see with my particular life experience," Glenn said, continuing to walk. "When I share that moment with people, I bear witness. Even something as small as watching an ant can be an enormous act of courage."

Magnus looked back down the street they had just walked. They were just at the edge of the city, and he could still easily return home. He doubted the wisdom of going anywhere with this eccentric man. At the same time, something about Glenn intrigued him. Magnus knew it might be because he was desperate, but he wanted to believe Glenn was speaking the truth.

"What is going to become of me?" Magnus asked, catching up with Glenn with several long strides. "What am I going to do if I'm not an accountant? What have you done with your life?"

"The less I tell you about myself, the better. I'm just one possibility of what your life might be. Nothing is set in stone. You can always change your future. It's a dangerous thing to think you know what your future is. Stronger men than you have been destroyed by knowing too much."

As Magnus pondered this, Glenn pointed to a dead tree with weathered branches at the side of the road. Three crows huddled close together on the shortest branch.

Magnus studied them, as if Glenn had told him those birds would reveal the meaning of life. However, he could see nothing significant. As he looked harder, trying to see what he might be missing, he suddenly remembered that as a boy, he had been interested in animal signs, especially when visiting his grandparents at their country home. He had learned in school that in ancient Greek and Roman times, an augur could interpret the flight of birds. They would decipher what it meant that there was a certain number of a particular type of bird in a specific place. They'd see significance in the crows flying off and the direction they went, and in how long they stayed close together.

As a child, Magnus had noticed that animals appeared at important events in his life. He had believed they were omens—until his friends and his parents laughed at him for being superstitious. By age eight, he had tucked this belief away and never spoke of it again, soon to forget it.

Now, he wondered if perhaps he had been right.

Astounded by this thought, Magnus stopped dead. Then he immediately dismissed it. Three crows were just three crows.

"What you do doesn't matter," Glenn said. "It is how you do it that is important. Carry love in each gesture of your life."

"That's nonsense."

"Suit yourself," Glenn said, placidly, stroking his beard.

As the men continued walking, Magnus decided Glenn knew nothing about the real world. He thought Glenn's pronouncements were over-simplifications of life.

"Simple truths don't need to be wrapped up in fancy ribbons and bows," Glenn said, as though he had just heard Magnus' thoughts. "Children see them and know them, when adults can't understand. I speak simply, but am never simplistic."

As they walked past the crows, Magnus couldn't quite dismiss the idea that he was meant to see them. They seemed to watch him intently. He was surprised to realize that their dark eyes on him made him feel less alone. However, when he noticed a single vulture flying overhead, he felt uneasy again. One of the crows cawed and then fell silent. An instant later,

Magnus thought he heard someone right behind him whisper in a low voice: *Fool.*

He jumped at the sound, but when he looked around, he saw no one. A sharp pain came and went through his knee.

"Did you hear that?" Magnus asked, rubbing his knee.

"What?"

"The voice. Someone called us—me—a 'fool.' "

"You must have heard the wind in the trees," Glenn said. "They speak, in their way. But never in human words."

"Where is this secret bookstore?" Magnus asked. He glanced back in the direction he had heard the voice and then turned back to Glenn. "Is the forest you live in much farther?"

"Don't worry. I know a short-cut out of the city," Glenn promised.

Even though Magnus noticed the old man had a tendency to avoid answering his questions, he decided to continue following Glenn, for his knee ached and less walking appealed to him. Then he visualized Matilda's beautiful face before him, and he felt a surge of energy and desire to continue onward.

The Postman

Glenn led Magnus through several unfamiliar back alleys. To his amazement, Glenn was right; within fifteen minutes they were out of the city and on a quiet dirt road far from the roaring traffic of the main highway. Here it did not smell of exhaust fumes, but of warm earth and damp leaves. Birdsong filled the air. Magnus' faith in this strange man grew a little, as he thought perhaps Glenn wasn't a lunatic after all.

"How can you see anything wearing those sunglasses?" Glenn said, stopping abruptly near a tree stump at the edge of the road. "May I see them?"

Magnus removed them, and handed them over. Before he knew what was happening, Glenn dropped them to the road and stomped on them, crushing them under his hiking boot.

Magnus slowly bent and picked up the broken pieces. He opened and closed his mouth several times before he said coldly, "I paid three hundred dollars for those glasses."

"You could afford to buy another dozen pairs."

Magnus gaped again. Glenn was right.

"That's not the point," Magnus protested. He pressed his lips together and tried not to reveal his anger. "That was unnecessary and unkind."

"Not really. I did you a favour. You'll see."

Glenn pointed above them. Magnus looked up at the bold blue sky. It was no longer a muted grey, as it had been with the glasses.

"You're not used to looking at things fully in the light. You have to get used to direct sunlight. On the way to the bookstore, you'll find shade when you need it. Too often people disregard shadows." Glenn stroked his beard. "You're angry."

"No," Magnus snapped. "I'm not angry."

Glenn turned and picked up two short, thick sticks and held them up.

"You need to do some drumming," he said.

Magnus knew what Glenn meant. When he was deeply upset and could not shut out his feelings— something that happened once or twice year— he played the drums. He had a set in a small room in his condo. He had had a professional sound-proof the room, so he wouldn't bother the neighbours. He'd play for minutes or hours, until the emotions flowed through him and dissipated.

The drums had belonged to his roommate in university. In the second year of school, after his roommate had killed himself, Magnus had felt only numb shock. But then he had picked up the drum sticks and started playing. As he did so, grief had flooded him. He kept playing through rage, fear, loneliness, tears and insomnia.

Magnus grabbed the sticks from Glenn and pounded a nearby tree stump. Decaying bits of wood flew off as he drummed against it. The sticks cracked and broke apart. After about five minutes, the anger over the sunglasses peaked, and then ebbed away. Glenn was right; he could buy dozens more pairs of sunglasses if he wanted. Feeling calm again, Magnus dropped the sticks and turned to Glenn.

"I'm ready to go on," he said.

Glenn did not smirk. Instead, he gave Magnus a small half-smile that was just as sad as it was happy. Magnus sighed inwardly as he realized that the journey wasn't going to be easy.

"At some point the journey will change for you," Glenn said. "It won't really get easier, but you'll accept things as they happen, as you understand the challenges."

"It's like you hear my thoughts." Magnus shivered.

"I remember what I was like fifty years ago. Truly, I've done a lot of changing. But you're still inside of me."

Walking onward down the road, they passed a field of ripening corn and several farm houses. Magnus had not left the city for years. The unfamiliar countryside with waving wildflowers, rustling grass and whirring grasshoppers was another world, holding the potential for mystery. This was a place where fairy tales might be real. He imagined that animals might dance and sing here, like in the movies. Then he glanced at Glenn from the corner of his eye, concerned the old man might have heard his thoughts and would laugh at him.

"Humans are always afraid of being laughed at," Glenn said. "As though that were some form of death. Why do people believe that animals only talk in the movies? Consider that the turkey vulture has no real voice. All it can do is grunt or hiss. But it talks to other vultures with a mere glance."

"Do you know why there were seven vultures sitting on my car?" Magnus asked. "And why was a mouse in my car this morning?"

"Truly, I couldn't say. Look there." Glenn pointed ahead with his wooden cane. "Let's see who he is. He looks like an interesting sort of fellow."

The road they walked on intersected with a narrow side road. At the corner a man in a blue postal uniform sat on a rocking chair, nestled in amongst dried grass, chicory and Queen Anne's lace. A large canvas sack rested beside him on his right. To his left sat a porcupine. The man wore leather gloves, which was fortunate, Magnus thought, as he was petting the porcupine. The animal grunted. A dank odour came from the creature, so Magnus tried to breathe through his mouth, not his nose, to avoid the stench.

"You've come to pick up your mail?" the postman asked. He stood up and removed his cap. "Please sit, while I look for your letters. Don't touch the porcupine. It doesn't like strangers."

The porcupine rattled its quills in agreement, as the postman returned his cap to his head. Magnus glanced around, looking for a post office or a car, some explanation of why the man was there. Then he brushed a hand across his forehead, again wondering if he had injured his brain in the car accident.

He noticed that Glenn was watching him closely. Magnus shrugged, as if to say he was able to accept the strangeness of the moment without fear of what was happening. He would prove to Glenn, and Matilda, that he was brave.

So far the day had been strange, and somehow he expected it to get stranger yet. But he wanted to believe that everything happening to him was real. Even more than real, like the water at the waterfront that had seemed like something in a movie. Then he realized that he felt like he was in a movie or novel, and that he liked the feeling.

The postman opened the sack and riffled through the envelopes and packages, as Glenn sat and rocked in his chair. Magnus removed his suit jacket and hung it over his arm as they waited. He stepped back, to avoid disturbing the porcupine, but the animal seemed uninterested in his presence. Its rounded body remained immobile, its small eyes staring straight ahead.

As he spread packages and letters around, the postman seemed disturbed that he couldn't find any mail for them. He held the sack upside-down and shook it. A lone letter fell out. He looked at that hopefully, but it wasn't addressed to them.

"Expecting something?" the postman asked sharply.

"No," Magnus said.

"Well!" the man exclaimed, raising his thick eyebrows. He tossed the empty sack to the ground.

At the postman's loud shout, the porcupine puffed out its quills. Glenn bent to look at it, and the animal tucked in its small head, thumped its back feet and swatted at him with its tail. Glenn jumped back, just avoiding being struck across his cheek.

"Why didn't you say so?" the postman said. He removed his cap and slapped his knee with it. "If you're not expecting anything, then there won't be anything here!"

Muttering to himself, the postman picked up the sack, grabbed a package, and thrust it in.

"I'm looking for a bookstore," Magnus said.

He showed him the business card for The Secret Bookstore, but the postman ignored him.

The postman mumbled to himself, "Not expecting anything. Imagine that… and probably always getting just the little you expect."

The postman shook his head and continued muttering, as he finished gathering and stuffing all the packages and letters into the sack. He tied it with a piece of twine and gestured for Glenn to move aside so he could sit on his rocking chair again.

Glenn leaned on his cane to stand up and thanked the man for the use of his chair.

Magnus' eyelid twitched nervously. He thought of the stories he would have to tell people when he got back home. He reached into his pants pocket for his cell phone to text someone. His hand touched the inside of his pocket and came out empty, as he remembered that he'd left the device in the office.

Then he realized that no one would believe him because he would sound crazy. He shrugged, like he had before. Something bubbled up inside of him that he thought felt like joy.

"I know it's been a long time since you've enjoyed yourself," Glenn said. "If you choose to see it as an adventure, this journey will be fun."

As Glenn patted Magnus' shoulder, Magnus sensed the shadow of a person moving to his right. He spun around to look, but all he saw were bulrushes waving in a ditch. Glenn seemed not to have noticed the shadow, so Magnus doubted he had seen anything at all. He pressed a hand to his throbbing knee, as Glenn patted his shoulder again.

"You're thinking this is a strange place I'm taking you to. Forget everything you thought you knew about the world and life, and you'll see even more wonderful things."

"Is that a promise or a warning?" Magnus asked.

"Time will tell," said Glenn. He looked into the distance, as though pondering the question and answer, stroking his beard.

"Truly, time will tell."

"Does time actually exist?" Magnus asked.

"Excellent question. You're a quick learner. I always liked that about myself. No, it doesn't exist. Not really."

Glenn chuckled, as Magnus wiped clammy hands on his suit pants and wondered if he had made the right choice to follow this old man out here.

"Desperate men take whatever opportunities appear to them," Glenn said, seeming to read his mind again.

Magnus nodded, relieved that he finally understood something Glenn said.

Dog Chase

They continued down the same road. After a few minutes of walking, the gravel road narrowed into a dirt road with deep ruts that meandered between fields of pale yellow barley. Glenn brushed the spikes of the ripe grain with his fingertips as they walked. Magnus imitated him, surprised how hard the dry barley felt against his skin. Glenn smelled his fingertips.

"Smells like almonds," he said.

Magnus imitated him, but could smell nothing on his fingers, except, perhaps, the memory of the forest that clung to the card that Matilda had given him.

He felt uneasy being so far from the city, from civilization. He didn't enjoy camping or hiking. Insects and spiders and snakes made his skin crawl. With his dress shoes pinching his toes and rubbing against the backs of his ankles, and wearing his suit, he was not prepared for a long walk. He kept thinking of his cell phone, feeling the urge to text someone or check the weather or complete a work project.

Just as Magnus was about to suggest they return to the city to rent a car to speed up the journey, in the distance several dogs snarled and barked. Glenn and Magnus paused to listen. The dogs sounded like they were moving closer.

"Run!" Glenn yelled.

They left the road, half-limping, half-sprinting along a ditch, and pushed through several red sumac trees. They came to a field of sunflowers and ran along its edge. As the barking grew louder, Magnus couldn't resist peeking over his shoulder. Two Rottweilers were chasing them, snapping their teeth as saliva speckled their muzzles. Magnus tried to run faster, but his bad knee and his out-of-shape, slightly overweight body prevented it. He was just keeping up with Glenn, and he was breathing far more heavily than the old man.

"How are you at climbing trees?" Glenn asked.

"I don't think I could," Magnus gasped. He couldn't remember the last time he had run anywhere, and he'd been a boy the last time he climbed a tree.

"Then throw them the chocolate bar in your suit pocket."

Magnus fumbled to pull the chocolate bar out, not pausing to ask Glenn how he knew it was there. It was what he ate for breakfast in the office most mornings. In the process of removing the chocolate, Magnus dropped the blank leather book that Glenn had given him. He stopped to snatch up the book, and continued running, just as the dogs reached his heels.

"Good work," Glenn said, as the dogs ripped the bar apart.

"Isn't chocolate poisonous for dogs?"

"You'd rather find and give them a steak? Or give them your leg to chew on? Keep going. We're almost there."

"The Secret Bookstore?" Magnus asked, hardly daring to hope they had found it already.

"Nope!" Glenn ran into a field of sunflowers. "Come on!"

They ran through the rough leaves and stems, scratching their hands and faces. The dogs crashed through the flowers behind them. Startled blue jays and gold finches scattered up into the air around them.

After a long minute of running, Glenn and Magnus burst through the field of sunflowers into a clearing with a horse stable, several sheds and a white wooden house. As they neared the front door, one of the dogs nipped the bottom of Magnus' pant leg, tearing a new hole there. A young man wearing a grey cap came out of a vegetable garden at the side of the house. He whistled once, and the dogs stopped barking and ran to sit on either side of him. The animals seemed to grin at Magnus, as their tongues lolled from the corners of their mouths, their sides heaving from the chase. One of them licked its lips, finding tiny bits of chocolate.

On the front porch, an old farmer played a banjo. He nodded at Magnus and Glenn, and kept playing as though he was not at all startled to see them running out of his field chased by dogs. Beside him a woman sat behind a spindle. She had a fluffy pile of white wool on her lap. She was pulling tufts of the wool from the pile and spinning it into yarn.

Glenn greeted these people like they were long-lost friends, hugging the young man.

"The dogs are sociable," the young farmer said to Magnus, as he shook his hand. "They were only playing a game of tag."

Too winded to speak, Magnus grumbled his disagreement. He remembered the feel of the dog at his ankles and pointed at his torn pant leg. He put his hands on his knees and kept his head down, trying to catch his breath. His sides ached.

"Who won?" the older farmer asked, still playing the banjo.

"Leave him be," the woman said.

Magnus looked more closely at the woman and her spinning. The ball of wool had an eye that opened slowly and blinked several times. Then he recognized the long ears and pink nose of an enormous Angora rabbit.

"It would have been easier if you had just invited us," Glenn said. "I was planning to come."

"The dogs brought you right here, didn't they?" the young farmer said. "And quickly."

"Was there a hurry?" Magnus asked, as he stood up.

No one answered. The old farmer continued plucking at the banjo, and his wife kept spinning. The rabbit's eyes both opened, looked drowsily at Magnus, and then closed again. Time seemed to stretch out like a long elastic band between them, no one willing to break the silent moment.

"Getting lost is part of the journey, right?" the young man asked finally.

"It always is," said Glenn.

"Do you know the way back to the city?" Magnus asked, as he glanced around. He was so completely lost that he'd only be able to find his way back home with help.

The young man, old farmer and his wife all shrugged. Magnus wondered about Glenn's words, and if getting lost had been part of Glenn's plan.

"Yes, it was part of the plan," Glenn said, with a smirk. "You're now completely dependent on me to guide you onward. You are in a different world now."

Magnus ground his teeth together. He hated feeling powerless and helpless. If he weren't so winded from the run, he would have grabbed two sticks and pounded out his anger on a tree trunk. Instead he pressed a hand to his aching side and tried not to grimace.

He could be safe in his office right now, his fingers flying over the computer keyboard or a calculator. Even as he considered this, his shoulders sagged at the thought of being back at work in the city.

Continuing on the journey with Glenn frightened him, and returning to his routine life frightened him. His mind had no easy answer for how he should proceed. He felt trapped within his own fears.

"How much farther to the forest?" Magnus asked.

"You don't want to turn back now do you?" Glenn asked him.

"Yes. No. I mean—," Magnus stammered. "I don't know."

Glenn stared hard into Magnus' eyes, like he had outside the condo building, seeming to look into his very soul. Uncomfortable, Magnus dropped his gaze to his feet. He noticed that his shoes were scuffed. His suit now had a hole in the elbow and at the bottom of his leg; he realized he didn't care about either.

Then he remembered the sound of Matilda's voice and the tinkling of her glass bead necklace. He visualized her eyes and full lips. His heart leapt at the remembrance of her. He crossed his arms and dug his fingers into his forearms. Instead of asking for help to go home, he would continue on with Glenn to the bookstore. His heart beat a little faster, and his chest swelled a little too, as he knew that today he had made one of the first courageous decisions in his adult life.

Buying Walking Sticks

Glenn asked the young man for new walking sticks. The man's face brightened and he nodded.

"I carve one walking stick a year," the young man said, as he led them to the shed behind the horse stables.

Magnus wrinkled his nose at the stench of horse manure. Noticing Magnus' reaction, the man lifted his nose in the air and inhaled deeply.

"The smell of nature," the young man said.

"Of life!" Glenn added.

"Smells like hell," Magnus said.

Glenn and the young man laughed.

"You get used to it," the young man promised. "Now as I was saying. I only make one walking stick a year. I don't like to work faster than that. Glenn, you've been gone a long time, so I have fifty for you to choose from."

Magnus thought the man was lying or joking, for he didn't look any older than twenty. But the young farmer's face remained serious and no one laughed now.

"Are you asking me to believe you're over fifty years old?" Magnus said.

"I'm asking you to consider the possibility," the young-looking farmer said.

Magnus narrowed his eyes and inched a little closer to Glenn.

"You're aging well," Magnus said, wryly. "Either you're a liar or mad."

"Possibly both, but I prefer eccentric and unique," the man said. "Pick a cane or stick."

Numerous canes and walking sticks lined the walls of the shed. Magnus tried out the various sizes and heights and colours. He settled on a walking stick made of chestnut wood that was of a comfortable height that felt both solid and flexible in his hand. Glenn exchanged his cane for a walking stick as well, something more appropriate for hiking over uneven terrain.

"Pay the man," Glenn said, after they left the shed.

Magnus patted his pockets. His wallet was gone.

"It must have fallen out of my pocket while we were running from the dogs." Magnus rubbed his right eye to stop its nervous twitching.

"We could do an exchange instead. What can you do?" the young farmer asked.

Magnus looked around, trying to see what he could do. He

could think of nothing besides his accounting skills.

"You could write him a poem," Glenn said gently.

"I'd accept a poem," the farmer said, nodding.

"A poem?" Magnus asked, exaggerating the surprise on his face. "I can't write a poem."

"Why not?" Glenn asked.

"Why not?" echoed the farmer.

"I'm not a poet," Magnus said firmly. His face flushed. He rubbed his forehead. "I'm an accountant."

As a boy, Magnus had wanted to be a poet, but his father had convinced him that his eye for detail meant that he should be an accountant. But throughout his entire life, words and phrases of poetry came to him without warning. If he didn't acknowledge them, they would haunt him day and night. To get the words to leave him alone, he wrote a poem each evening in his condo. Then, without reading it again, he always destroyed the poem in a paper shredder because he was not a real poet.

He thought writing poetry was a vice like any other; no different than men who each evening smoked a cigar, or had a few drinks, or watched porn, or ate a bag of chips or an entire pizza. No one had to know, and no one had known. He just made it a part of his routine.

Magnus avoided Glenn's eyes, looking at his dirty shoes and shuffling in place. Magnus felt exposed.

"Or clean out the horse stables," Glenn said, gently.

"Agreed," the young farmer agreed. "Make your choice."

Magnus thought they were joking, but when they kept looking at him expectantly, he chose to clean out the stables.

While Glenn visited with the family in the house, the banjo music faintly drifting to the barn, Magnus shovelled horse manure. Blisters formed on his hands and his back ached. As he blinked sweat from his eyes, he knew that this was definitely not his purpose.

He longed to be in his office, forgetting that, minutes ago, he had been glad not to be there. The office chair was soft, and there'd be no physical labour in a smelly barn. He had gotten so many raises, awards and compliments for his quick and accurate work that he had grown to believe he was only and always meant to be an accountant.

He sighed, stopped shoveling and leaned against the barn wall. He suddenly understood that exactly because he had become so good at being an accountant, he had not realized how much he hated it. The harder he worked, the more assignments he took on, the less time he had to think about anything besides work, to feel lonely, to feel sad, to feel anything at all. People admired and respected his abilities at work, and that had satisfied him. Because he was bored and felt unhappy when he was home and not working, he believed that he must love his work. But now he understood that he didn't like it any more than shoveling horse manure.

When the newly formed blister on his hand popped and he touched his sweaty forehead with it, getting salt in his wound, Magnus winced and dropped the shovel. He decided that he would offer the man a poem for the walking stick so he could stop working here.

He pulled a pen out of his suit jacket and opened his new blank book to the first page. He glanced up. There were three turkey vultures circling overhead. His hand trembled as he wrote:

Saturation

the sky
        is filled

with
        just
                three turkey
vultures

The farmer had not specified how long the poem should be, so Magnus decided these words would be enough.

As he walked back to the house, a low, rough voice said: *Coward.*

Magnus froze. Again he saw no one, but this time he did

not doubt that he had heard someone. A sharp pain pierced through his knee, as it had every other time he'd heard the voice.

Go back home, the voice said.

Magnus spun around. He saw a chipmunk darting away from him.

"I don't know who you are," Magnus said, in a whisper. "But I am not a coward. And I will not go home now."

No one answered him. He jumped when two more chipmunks ran away from him over dried leaves. Shaking his head, Magnus thought about how he was now speaking to mysterious voices and shadows. He shook his head again, harder this time, as though that would settle his thoughts and nerves. The sharp pain disappeared from his knee, leaving just a dull ache.

He returned to the farmhouse, ripped the page out of the journal and gave the poem to the young farmer.

"This is the first poem that I've shared with someone else," Magnus said, softly and nervously.

After reading the poem with a smile, the young farmer thanked Magnus with a deep bow, and told Glenn and Magnus they were free to leave with their walking sticks.

Magnus' suit smelled like manure, and now had mud and manure stains on it. There was a rip at the elbow and a tear at his ankle. But there was a small part of him that felt whole, content and joyful for having written a poem and sharing it.

The feeling surprised him.

He was certain that now he was no longer a cliché. He liked this feeling, too.

Buzzing Bees

Magnus and Glenn limped away from the farm. Glenn stopped abruptly near a stand of trees, got down on his hands and knees and pointed out a slight bend in the grass.

"Deer recently walked here," Glenn said.

Magnus bent over and studied the spot Glenn pointed at, but only saw grass. He wanted to see what Glenn saw, and stared so hard that the blades all blurred into one green blob. Glenn pushed aside a handful of grass.

"Deer dung," Glenn said.

Magnus jumped backwards.

"And here is a coyote print," Glenn said, gleefully. "We'll track that. It looks like a dog's print, but the front paw is larger than the back and their toes are closer together than a dog's. Prints are easiest to follow in the snow, but even now I'll find markings on plants and in the ground. Come, I'll show you."

"But why track a coyote? Aren't we going to the forest to find The Secret Bookstore?" Magnus rubbed his forehead in puzzlement.

"If you want to track, you have to notice even the smallest signs," Glenn said.

"Does the bookstore move around like a wild animal?"

Glenn leaned onto his walking stick as he stood up. "The Secret Bookstore isn't looking to be found. You're going to have to hunt it. Track it. Through the process you might prove yourself worthy of a book. Truly, to do that you must start paying attention. This journey will be a challenge. But there are a few rewards. Here and there."

"I think we should get some proper supplies," Magnus said. "A compass and fresh water and snacks. Some local maps. Maybe I could go back and rent a car."

"All we need will be provided on the journey." Glenn waved his cane around. "Truly, right now you don't notice your surroundings or see all the provisions that are already here because your mind is always busy. You're thinking about your next work project. Or thinking about the next work meeting, or planning what you want to buy."

"That's not true." Magnus frowned in disagreement. He hated people telling him how he supposedly thought or felt.

"It's as though there's a hive of bees inside your mind, buzzing constantly." Glenn tapped the ground several times with his cane. "The buzzing makes it hard for you to see or notice anything else. You think that the buzzing bees prove you are alive. But they merely distract you."

"Buzzing? You mean like a headache?"

"I mean bees buzzing." Glenn looked in the distance, as though trying to decide how to explain the concept, while he tugged the end of his beard. "If they stopped buzzing, you would have to feel something. And if they stopped buzzing, you would look around you, and then you would see a world so beautiful that you would sit down and weep."

"I never cry." Magnus straightened his back and lifted his chin, standing stiffly, with his shoulders squared, like his mother had taught him to sit at the supper table. He ignored the pain shooting out of his knee, determined not to shift in place.

"When the buzzing stops, your world will be still," Glenn responded. He tapped his index finger once on the top of his cane. "So time will seem to hesitate and you'll understand how I could be here. Then you will see that time does not exist, except in your imagination. You'd pause to accept what the moment offers you. You'd become like the vulture."

Magnus shuddered when Glenn mentioned the vulture. His knee nearly gave way and he loosened his back and bent over the walking stick. Magnus looked down and saw a ladybug climbing up the stick. The ladybug reached his index finger and continued walking, tickling the back of his hand. He believed Matilda would have appreciated the tiny, red insect and upon thinking of her, hoping to see her again, Magnus agreed they should go onward.

The Watch-Repairman

Mid-afternoon, after an hour of tracking the coyote through fields and shrubs and along the edge of a stand of trees, Magnus saw a slender man dressed in a midnight blue robe, looking like he came from a different century, walking towards them. He was hunched over and leaned to the right. As a walking stick, he used a crooked tree branch that was as tall as he was.

"I'm Vincent," he said, when he arrived, and shook each of their hands in turn. He had to turn his entire body to look straight at Magnus and Glenn. He had slicked back his thick grey hair from his forehead and it just touched the collar of his robe.

"My spine twists and turns where it wants," Vincent said, with a shrug. "Sort of like time itself. The doctor calls it scoliosis. Look, even my walking stick is slightly curved. Few things in my life are straight-forward."

Vincent laughed and wheezed simultaneously at his play on words.

"See, even my teeth lean where they want to," Vincent said, smiling and revealing a mouth full of crooked teeth.

Vincent wore four watches on each arm. One on his right wrist was a plastic child's watch.

"I repair them," Vincent said, turning to look directly at Magnus, who was studying all the watches. "After fixing one, I always wear it for a day to be sure it's working properly, before returning it to the customer. I've got too much time on my arms. But no time constraints."

Vincent wheezed and laughed again at his own joke. His laughter turned to coughing, leaving him bent over so far that his head almost touched the ground. Magnus glanced down at the Cartier watch on his own arm. He decided now was not the time to point out that it was by far the most expensive of all of the watches there.

Once he stopped coughing and stood as straight as he could, Vincent said: "Why don't you follow me? I'll show you my watch repair shop just down the path."

"We don't have time," Magnus protested. "We're on the way to The Secret Bookstore."

"Time is an illusion," said Glenn. "The day will pause here."

"What? The sun will stand still?" Magnus asked, and laughed, glancing up at the sun glowing in the clear sky.

"We might learn something useful here," Glenn said, punctuating his words by stabbing the air with his walking stick.

After a brief hesitation, Magnus reluctantly agreed to follow Vincent, sensing he had little say in the matter anyway.

"I used to be a chef," Vincent said, wheezing loudly as he walked with them. "My father repaired watches, and when he retired I took over his shop. This job seemed more important. Now I give time back to people."

"Time is impossible to return to anyone, for it doesn't exist," Glenn said.

"True," Vincent said. "It's a human construct. However, I have observed that people demand the constraints of time. They like to be contained by schedules and watches and clocks and deadlines. People want to wrestle and fight with something to distract themselves from themselves. So they fight with the rules of time."

"How do you fight the rules of time?" Magnus asked. "Seems useless to me."

"People are senseless beings," Vincent said. "They actually think they can be late or early. Impossible! They arrive when they arrive."

"I'd get in trouble if I was late for work," Magnus said. "There'd be anarchy. What about bus schedules? The start of tax season?"

Vincent shook his head, and wheezed in disagreement. "Human constructs. To be free of time would be a burden for most people. Once they were free they would have to deal with themselves. So I let them continue to live in their illusion."

Vincent paused to cough. He then continued walking and wheezing. On the way to his shop they found a pear tree at the side of the road. Bees and wasps droned around the dozens of ripened yellow pears that had fallen to the ground. The men paused and picked a few pieces of ripe fruit from the tree.

Glenn pointed out a pair of blue boy's socks on top of a nearby bush, and with a chuckle took them and tucked them into one of his numerous jacket pockets. Magnus glanced around, looking for the child who might have owned them, but saw no one.

Then he looked up, half-wondering if indeed the sun was standing still, as though his looking for The Secret Bookstore was an event of Biblical magnitude. He blushed at his arrogance, even as he noticed how brightly the sun glowed, seemingly even stronger than it had just minutes ago.

"It's watching you," Vincent said.

"The sun?" Magnus asked.

"Yes. Doesn't it seem like it's curiously looking at us?" Glenn said.

Magnus blinked as he shaded his eyes with his hand and tried to look at the sun for a second or two before looking away. He wished he had his sunglasses.

"It's too strong. It almost feels violent." He touched his face and felt how hot it was. He raised his eyebrows and noticed his forehead was tight. "And this sunburn hurts like a wound."

"In a few weeks you'll be as tanned as me," Glenn said. "Then you'll blend into the woods, like me, like another tree. It will make you a better animal tracker. This morning you were so pasty it looked like you hadn't seen the sun in years."

"I haven't," Magnus said with a grimace.

He took out his leather book and jotted down: *The sun is violent in its brightness.*

"One day you'll wake up and look and sound just like me and wonder how it happened," Glenn said to Magnus.

"Tattoos and all?" Vincent asked, leaning heavily on his walking stick. "I can't imagine this here man in a suit decorated with tattoos."

"Wouldn't we argue all the time—don't we always fight with ourselves?" Magnus asked.

"Truly, you're right. You're a fast learner." Glenn patted Magnus' shoulder. "Wisdom is sure to follow."

The men were silent for a moment as they each pondered this.

"Let's go on. We're almost at my store," Vincent said. "There's shade there."

How Time Works

They ate the pears as they walked the rest of the way along a narrow path between a field of wheat and a wooded area. Magnus had not eaten anything yet that day, and pears had never tasted so delicious.

They arrived at an open field with a huge tree in the centre. A door and four windows had been built into the tree that Vincent said was his store.

"Here we enter into timelessness," Glenn said, with a sigh, as Vincent brought them inside. "Feels like heaven."

"Feels like home," Vincent added.

At the entranceway a television was on. The screen showed a clock, the second hand ticking around and around a white face. As he watched the video, Magnus' eyes glazed over and he fell into a sort of stupor, until Glenn tugged him from the TV.

"Thank you," Magnus said, sensing that he might never have been able to pull himself away.

Dozens of clocks on the walls of the inside of the tree

ticked steadily around them. A few glass display counters held watches. Before Magnus had time to look around more closely, Vincent asked: "Do you know why each minute has sixty seconds and each hour sixty minutes? Why not a hundred minutes per hour and a hundred seconds per minute?"

"I never thought about that," Magnus said.

"It was because of the Babylonians." Vincent tapped the child's watch with his index finger. "They had a base unit of sixty, not a hundred. That concept hasn't changed for thousands of years."

"No one tried changing the system to a base unit of a hundred?" Magnus asked.

"I read somewhere that the French tried it after their Revolution," Vincent said, leaning his tall stick against the wall beneath the many clocks. "It didn't work. But since then no one else has made such a grand attempt. No one dares. And now it would require a radical change in thinking. People who think about transforming the system tell themselves that it's too late. They believe no one would accept this new idea now. They don't realize nothing is ever too late, when you don't believe in time."

"True enough," Glenn said.

"I'll tell you a secret," Vincent whispered, leaning close to Magnus and Glenn. "I'm tinkering with a clock based on a hundred seconds per minute. It works brilliantly. When people are ready, I'm going to market it."

In a display of exuberance, Vincent did a little tap dance. Glenn joined in. Magnus raised his eyebrows, again noticing his sunburnt skin.

"Could I apprentice here?" Magnus asked, surprising himself with his impulsive question.

Glenn and Vincent froze mid-dance.

"I mean—." Magnus stuttered and stopped, unsure what he really *did* mean.

"Yes, you could. But first you have to understand how time works," Vincent said, shifting his blue robe and wrapping it more tightly around himself, and turning to look directly at Magnus.

"You mean how a watch works?" Magnus asked.

"No. I mean how time works."

"I don't understand," Magnus said. He lightly rubbed a hand across his forehead that was creased in puzzlement.

Vincent took off all eight watches from his arms and laid them in a row on a glass display counter at the back of the shop.

"Time bends and folds and twists and doubles back, and moves right alongside of life. If you want to escape time, you have to understand how it works," said Vincent, looking shrewdly at Magnus.

Magnus was silent, as he wondered to himself if Vincent's words explained the presence of Glenn and if it was really possible Glenn was his future-self.

"Leave your watch here and I'll repair it," Vincent said.

Magnus looked down at it. The second hand moved steadily around the face. "It's not broken."

Vincent held out his hand. Magnus removed his Cartier watch and handed it to him. Vincent held it to his ear for a half a minute and then passed it back.

"No, it's not broken." Vincent smiled, revealing his mouthful of crooked teeth. "But it could be improved and run more smoothly."

Magnus placed it on the counter top with the others, but did not remove his hand from it.

"All right, keep it," Magnus said, speaking slowly.

"Congratulations, Magnus," Glenn said. "You'll no longer have the burden of this illusion. You won't need it where we're going."

"If the time is right, we might meet again," Vincent said, laughing and wheezing.

With a sinking feeling, Magnus realized he might never see his watch again, as he put his hand in his pocket and left the watch on the counter top.

"Now you can start fresh, without any time constraints," Glenn said. "You'll never feel like you wasted a moment. You'll never be late or early. You'll be right where you are, without having to get anywhere. The journey will be neither long nor short."

"Before you go, I have some clothes for you, if you'd like

them," Vincent said to Magnus.

He showed Magnus a trunk packed with old jeans, faded t-shirts and worn jackets and shoes. Magnus glanced from them to his stained and smelly business suit, and decided to keep on his own clothes.

"Suit yourself," Glenn said, again laughing with Vincent at his play on words.

There was a light knock at the door. A young boy's voice piped up from outside, audible through one of the open windows:

"Glenn! Magnus! Wait! Don't leave without me."

The Child

A young boy, around seven years old, carrying a metal pail and wearing a shiny blue birthday hat, stood in the doorway. His shoes hung from their laces around his neck. He wore jeans, and a midnight blue T-shirt that was the same colour as Vincent's robe. His feet were bare.

"I wondered if you'd be invited," Glenn said, as he picked up and hugged the slender child. As he did so, the boy's birthday cap fell off. Glenn ruffled the child's already tussled blonde hair. "I found your socks on a bush."

Magnus wondered who would have invited the boy, and if he himself had been invited on the journey. Or perhaps he had been summoned. But summoned to what purpose? And by whom? He felt agitated, until he considered that maybe Matilda had summoned him. He felt warmth at the idea that she might want him to find her.

"I came from a birthday party," the boy said, picking his hat up from the ground and throwing it into the air. He caught it as it came down, and put it back on his head.

"I love parties," Glenn said, grinning at the boy. "Every day is a like a birthday party, isn't it?"

"Yes. Hey, look up there," the boy said. He pointed up at three vultures circling above the watch-repair shop. "They're like giant needles knitting the sky into place."

Magnus thought the child's words sounded like a poem. He opened his leather book and scribbled down the sentence about the knitting needles.

"Please, introduce yourself," Vincent said to the boy.

The boy reached out and shook Magnus' large hand with his own small, sticky one. Magnus tried not to grimace as he pulled his hand away and wiped it on his pants.

The boy looked shyly at his feet, as he mumbled that he had been eating birthday cake.

"This is your younger self," Glenn informed Magnus.

The boy pointed at the empty space beside him. "And this is my best friend, Robin."

"And you're coming with us to the forest?" Magnus asked, not quite managing to keep the incredulity from his voice. He looked beyond the boy down the path that led away from Vincent's shop.

The boy whispered to the empty space beside him. He paused, as though listening for an answer.

"Yes. And Robin is coming too," the child declared. He reached into the metal pail that he had set down, and held out both his hands. In one he held a worm, in the other a salamander. "They're coming too. Here, smell." He stretched his hand out towards Magnus.

The boy's open face and bold eyes shone with the innocence and trust of a child who had not been frightened or forced to grovel for forgiveness. Magnus took the worm and salamander from his hands. They felt cool on his skin. He sniffed them. Their earthy smell was not as unpleasant as he expected.

Magnus glanced up to study the boy, to see if there was any resemblance to himself as a child. The child smiled at Magnus, while Magnus studied him.

Magnus hadn't looked at childhood photos for many years and while he could not say he had forgotten how he looked, he didn't exactly remember either. He hadn't thought of his childhood for a long time; perhaps, his hair had once been sun-bleached and his skin been as tanned as this boy's. He noted that he, the boy and Glenn had the same deep blue eyes.

"They smell like dirt," Magnus said finally, and handed the worm and salamander back to the child.

"Of course they do." The boy grinned as he dropped the creatures back into the pail. He patted his bulging jean pockets. He pulled out a pink pebble and white rock and held them up for Magnus to see. "I've got lots of rocks!" He tossed the two he had just removed from his pockets into the pail. Then he pressed the pointed birthday hat more tightly on his head.

"I'm glad you were still here," the boy added.

"You're right on time," Glenn pronounced. "Neither a moment too early nor too late."

"Which way are we going?" the boy asked.

Glenn pointed down a path along a fence.

"Wait," Vincent said, putting a hand on the boy's head. "Have some cookies before you go. I have your favourite: chocolate chip. What's a visit without cookies?"

"Yippee!" the boy shouted.

Vincent went into a back room of his shop, and returned with a jar that had been painted with the face of a clock, including black eyes and smiling thin red lips. The boy reached in and took some cookies. Magnus and Glenn followed his lead. Magnus gobbled down several in a row. The boy took a few more. Vincent nodded at Magnus, so Magnus took out another handful, eating ravenously.

"Have some more," Vincent urged when Magnus had finished the second helping of cookies.

Magnus reached in and found only one cookie left. He flushed, and apologized for eating them all.

"Why not write a poem as thanks?" Glenn said.

"Gratitude is as a good a gift as any," Vincent said.

Magnus hesitated. This would be the second poem he'd share with someone. While he still felt apprehensive, it did not feel as nerve-wracking as when he shared his writing with the young farmer in exchange for his walking stick.

He pulled his leather book from his suit jacket pocket and wrote down:

Gratitude

the cookie
        jar is

empty
       because the

cookies
        were
                so

delicious

He re-read the words several times, until he was sure that he was content with what he had written. Then he copied the words onto a scrap of paper that Vincent handed him, and gave the poem to Vincent.

"It's short. Not much at all," Magnus apologized. "But it's all I have to say."

"You're more than welcome," Vincent said.

"The simplest compliment is the best," Glenn said, patting Magnus' shoulder. "I couldn't have said it better myself."

Two Things To Know, Three That Are Useful

The boy picked up his metal pail, and then ran on bare feet down the path that Glenn had pointed out earlier. Although quick and flexible, like a cat, he nearly ran into an oak sapling, swerving out of the way at the last moment.

"He's just like you—clumsy," Glenn said. "And his arms and legs are slightly too long, out of proportion to his body, like us."

"How can that boy be me?" Magnus demanded, feeling free to speak about the child now that he was out of hearing.

"How can Glenn be your older self?" Vincent asked.

"That doesn't make sense either. Nothing of this makes sense."

Magnus cleared his throat. He pressed his right eye to stop it from twitching. Then he closed both his eyes. Perhaps he was in a dream.

But when he opened them, he was still standing there beside Glenn. The boy was still traipsing on the path ahead.

None of this made sense, but it was not a dream. He felt as if he were trapped in a fairy tale, or in a tall tale that someone was telling friends at a bar. And some small part of him was enjoying the experience.

"There are two things you should know," Glenn said. "Three things that will be useful to you. First, don't we constantly talk to ourselves? How is this different? Here I am. Here is the child. We'll talk together, much like a lively conversation in your mind.

"Second, you are in a tale. That's true.

"The third thing, the most important to remember, would be for you to try to have fun as we journey onwards. It's not so bad out here, is it?"

"It's not so bad," Magnus said, half-lying to himself and Glenn.

He squinted at the sun, thinking of his broken sunglasses. He touched his bare wrist, naked without his watch. He glanced back into the store at the glass counter where it was lying. He patted his suit pant pockets that had neither wallet nor cell phone. He sniffed, smelling horse manure on his clothes.

"But we can't just take a stray child with us as if we'd found a dog," Magnus insisted.

"We have to take care of him until he's taught you all you need to know," Glenn responded.

"What's a boy going to teach me?" Magnus threw his hands up in the air.

Not far down the path ahead of them, the boy stopped and peered into hole in a tree. He put both the worm and salamander in the hole.

"I can pick them up when we come back," the boy shouted.

As Magnus watched and gaped, the boy scrambled up the tree. He stopped and nestled into the crook of a thick branch, and waved at them.

"We have to get him down," Magnus hissed to Glenn.

"He'll find his own way," Glenn answered. "He's blessed. Afraid of neither life nor death."

"He should be afraid of falling and killing himself."

"Go ahead." Glenn gestured at the boy. "Teach him fear. Make him as fearful as you are."

Magnus opened and then closed his mouth, unsure how to answer. He limped quickly from Vincent's shop to the tree, prepared to coax the child to the ground. Just as he stood under the tree, the child began to climb back down. As he did so, his bare foot slipped against a slender branch that broke under his weight. Magnus dropped his walking stick and caught the boy as he tumbled through the air.

With a giggle the boy jumped out of Magnus' arms and to the ground. The birthday hat fell off again. He picked it up and he put it on, this time making sure the elastic was snug under his chin.

"Thanks!" the boy said, looking up at him with wide eyes

for a brief moment, before running ahead again.

"If he is me, did I just save myself from premature death?" Magnus asked Glenn, who came up beside him with Vincent. "If he had died, would we both have died?"

"Like I've said, you have your own path," Glenn said. "The boy and I are just possibilities. We might be able to help you find your best new future."

"You have endless choices ahead," Vincent said. "And plenty of time for all of them."

"But will I change my past if I speak with him? And change myself, or you, by changing the boy?" With his walking stick he tapped an oak tree, as ahead the boy hit a huge maple tree trunk with a twig.

"He's just one version of what we could have been," Glenn said. "There are lots of choices. One choice doesn't preclude another. Sometimes roads lead up ahead. Other times they trail behind you and show you old choices that you can still make."

"Listen to this man. He knows what he's talking about," Vincent said.

"And I don't know how long I'll be around to help you, so the child will show you what I can't," Glenn said.

"What do you mean you don't know how long you'll be around?" Magnus asked, alarmed. "Are you leaving me? Are you—are you dying?"

Glenn pointed at the sky with his cane. "We know the sun always sets. So, of course I'll die. We know the time when the sun sets. But some days feel long and some feel short. I don't know the length of my day. But I'm closer to the end than to the beginning. Look at me. Truly, this is not the face of a young man."

Before Magnus could respond, Glenn left him standing there and continued walking after the child.

"Goodbye, Vincent," Glenn said, casually, over his shoulder. "Until next time."

Vincent and Glenn laughed.

Ahead of them, the boy paused and leapt into a puddle, sending water flying everywhere, getting both himself and Glenn wet. Glenn laughed loudly and splashed the boy back.

Magnus said goodbye to Vincent and followed these two people claiming to be him, as his eye twitched again. Uncertainty filled him. He thought if he were sane, he'd abandon Glenn and the boy and find a way to return to his condo and his old life, where everything was predictable and logical and orderly. But his heart shouted at him to have faith. Magnus stopped and leaned on his walking stick to still both his heart and mind.

He realized that he wanted to believe Glenn was his older self, and the boy his younger self! He admired Glenn and his endless practical skills. He liked the self-confident man he supposedly would become over fifty years. While the circular conversations with Glenn were infuriating, they also fascinated him.

A shout of triumph from the boy interrupted his thoughts. Ahead of them, the boy was on his hands and knees, peering into a hollow at the base of another tree. He reached in a hand and triumphantly held it up. He ran to Magnus to show him a tiny snail that fit on the tip of his pinkie finger. The boy handed Magnus the snail and ran on. As Magnus studied the tiny creature, trying to see the wonder that the boy saw, his eye stopped twitching and his heart stopped pounding. Ahead, Glenn and the boy walked hand in hand, Glenn leaning on his walking stick and the boy swinging his pail. A turkey vulture flew directly above them.

Magnus felt a sharp pang at the boy's innocence. Although he could not remember being as innocent as this, a faint memory of his own childhood arose through the thick fog of his forgetting. As a boy, he had caught a snail and kept it for a day in a pail at the back door of his house before letting it go at his mother's insistence. And then, he was startled to have arise a vague memory of himself climbing trees in his backyard when his mother wasn't looking. He had inhaled the scent of pine needles and pretended it was Christmas in July.

Oh, he thought, his heart painfully tight in his chest. *I hope the boy doesn't become like me.*

Elliott

Because the child refused to tell them his real name and Magnus refused to keep calling him "boy," Magnus decided to name him Elliott, his maternal grandparents' last name. Something about the child reminded him of the grandfather. His grandfather had been a carefree, easy-going man, always ready to laugh.

The boy nonchalantly accepted the name, and Glenn commented that it suited him.

"Besides," Glenn said. "We'd get confused calling each other Magnus, wouldn't we?"

When Magnus asked the boy where he had come from, Elliott whispered into the air beside him, speaking to Robin. As he did so, Magnus recollected that when he was a child he had believed he was always being followed by an angel. Once, he was sure the angel saved him from being hit by a car. When he told his mother this, she sternly told him to remember he was already seven and too old for imaginary friends. After this, the angel appeared less frequently, until Magnus never saw it again.

Magnus thought he must have had a good imagination, like Elliott.

The child darted ahead and bent down to look at something on the ground. Triumphantly, he held up a small snake.

"Look," Elliott said. "It's a beauty!"

Magnus pretended to smile, but was relieved when Elliott put the reptile in his pail, and didn't come closer with it. Then the boy picked up a stick and hit it against every tree he passed. It was as if he needed to touch or hit things to know their essence, to know what was really there, as if just seeing something wasn't enough.

Magnus noted that the boy's clothes looked normal, and this relieved him. As a child, Magnus' mother had sewed all his clothes for him. She deliberately made them several sizes too large, so he could grow into them. All his shirts had been too long. He had had to roll up his sleeves and pant cuffs for two years, before they fit. Not until Magnus was eight, and had insisted on doing a paper route so he could earn money to buy new clothes, did he look like the other children, and school and life became easier for him. That was when he had first experienced the pleasure of earning, saving and spending money.

Glenn came up beside Magnus, and they walked on together. Magnus touched the smooth bark of a poplar tree that Elliott had hit with a stick.

"Won't his parents worry about him?" Magnus asked.

"Sure enough, as long as he's here, he'll take care of us."

Magnus puzzled over Glenn's words, but before he could ask more questions Elliott ran to them with an orange and black caterpillar he had found.

"You're a born tracker," Glenn said, stroking his beard. "I'm going to teach you how to track all kinds of animals. I saw some coyote prints over there."

Elliott cheered. Then he dropped the caterpillar in his metal pail, took out the snake and set it carefully on the ground, and ran ahead.

Throughout the day, Magnus watched and listened as Glenn taught Elliott how to follow the coyote tracks.

Glenn taught the boy to walk lightly, to avoid twigs and sticks so he wouldn't startle animals as they approached. Elliott immediately understood, and in fact it seemed he hardly touched the earth, soon moving as silently on the path as vultures gliding in the sky.

As Magnus hovered nearby, Glenn told Elliott the names of plants he called pigweed, yellow rocket, Joe Pye Weed and pennycress. The names were so unusual to his ears, Magnus wondered if Glenn was inventing them to pique Elliott's interest. Glenn collected the leaves of chicory, pulled up burdock roots and gathered garlic mustard seeds that he put in various pockets of his jacket and the canvas sack he carried over his shoulder. He picked several mushrooms that he assured them were safe to eat, and wrapped them in a red handkerchief and added that to his sack as well. He pointed out a thistle and stinging nettle, and said the roots were also edible, but regretted that he didn't have a shovel to dig them up.

The list of plants that Glenn pointed out grew. Although Magnus tried to pay attention, they all looked identical to him, and he couldn't remember which were edible and which were poisonous, or which parts could be eaten raw and which should be cooked to make them less bitter or which were best in the fall or spring.

As the old man lectured, Magnus' mind kept wandering to all the food in his kitchen, longing for anything to eat, even a can of ravioli or Spam. He liked being prepared for any emergency. To that end, he had half a year's supply of canned and dried foods crammed into his kitchen cupboards. He ate very little of it, mostly eating take-out meals. But the emergency hoard made him feel safe, should any type of disaster strike.

In contrast, it seemed easy for Elliott to remember everything Glenn told him. But what really fascinated the boy were animals and rocks. His face brightened when he saw spiders, snakes and skating water bugs. He tried to take everything along and quickly filled his pail with natural treasures. When his pail overflowed, he removed an item or two, and handed it to Magnus or Glenn, and replaced it with something new. Magnus kept several stones and put them in his pockets. Each living creature that Elliott gave him, he carefully set back on the earth.

When they came across a large puddle of water, Elliott glanced quickly at Glenn before jumping. Glenn did not try to stop him. After Elliott jumped in, Glenn did not scold him for getting dirty or making so much noise. Instead, Glenn stomped in the puddle with him and they laughed together. And when Elliott's birthday hat fell in the puddle and got muddy, they only laughed harder. Elliott put the hat on his head, water and dirt running down his face, and they laughed harder still.

At the sidelines Magnus felt old and boring as he watched the old man and young child splashing each other. He especially admired how Elliott was completely fearless of water. He tried to remember when his own fear of water had begun, and came up blank.

Magnus wondered when he had started trying so hard to assimilate in society and become so colourless. He remembered that his father had been a composed man, so Magnus never knew what he was thinking or feeling. When he was a young child, his father often told him that only hysterical women or simpletons displayed their emotions and encouraged Magnus to hide his feelings behind a blank mask. Magnus now wondered that if along with hiding his feelings from people, he had suppressed and hidden them even from himself.

He liked that in this moment, he felt a flicker of joy while watching the old man and the young boy playing. He felt nostalgic for something he almost remembered, but he knew he could not be remembering, because it had never happened. Just as when he met Matilda, he felt as if he were remembering the future.

Resting For The Evening

Late in the afternoon, Glenn said, "We've gone far enough today. Time to rest and eat. You've both done well. Magnus, you've done far better than I remember myself doing at your age. We've had a very successful day."

"But we didn't find the coyote," Magnus pointed out, surprised that Glenn thought the tracking was a success. "And have we even made any progress? Are we any closer to the forest with The Secret Bookstore?"

"Look at the vultures," Glenn said. "They move in ever-widening and shrinking circles. Are they moving forward or backward, or anywhere at all? I doubt they've ever taken a perfectly direct route anywhere."

The skin at the back of Magnus' neck crawled. He scratched his neck, and picked off a yellow caterpillar that he dropped to the ground.

"Surely, you didn't expect to find the bookstore in one day?" Glenn asked.

Elliott giggled at the question and Magnus remained silent, trying to keep himself from glowering with anger, not wanting to lose his temper in front of the boy.

Glenn led Magnus and Elliott to a weathered barn on a ridge overlooking a creek.

"Our grand accommodations," Glenn said, sweeping out a hand. "Fit for a king."

"Awesome!" Elliott shouted, and ran to the barn to explore.

"A barn!" Magnus said, his voice rising. He took a deep breath and lowered his voice. "I'm not sleeping in a barn."

"Then join me on the ground beside the fire. We'll sleep under the stars." Glenn pointed up at the sky with his walking stick. With his other hand, he raised the rabbit that he had snared late that afternoon and had been carrying along with him. "We'll have a supper of rabbit stew. It will be delicious. I'm a great cook."

In anger and disgust Magnus turned away from Glenn, and followed Elliott to go and look inside the barn. Inside he found several piles of dry hay. Elliott jumped in one and a cloud of dust rose around him. The barn smelt of a decaying animal, and Magnus thought he saw a lump of matted fur in one corner. Nearly gagging from the stench and the dust, Magnus grabbed Elliott's hand, and dragged him out of the building. Glenn stood at the doorway as they tumbled outside.

"I think we should go home for the night," Magnus said.

He spoke slowly, enunciating each word clearly. It was how he spoke when his nerves were frazzled, but he was trying to maintain an exterior calm.

"Please, can't we stay?" Elliott begged. "Please."

Magnus looked from Glenn to Elliott, and then turned and took several steps back. He paused and realized neither one of them was following him. His knee throbbed; the pain begged him to sit and rest. He patted his empty suit pocket again, as he had many times that day. If he had had his cell phone, he would have called someone to pick him up.

"This is a perfect place for the night," Glenn called after him. "There's shelter here in the barn, if we want it. Or there's the ground with the stars above us all night. It's close to paradise."

"The ground?" Magnus said, speaking slowly again, drawing each word out. "And with no sleeping bag or blanket or pillow? I stink of sweat and horse manure. I could use a hot shower."

"Yes, you could. You do stink. But there's the creek to bathe in tonight," Glenn said, as he entered the barn. "And if I remember right, there should be everything we need under that tarp there."

Magnus watched him from the doorway as Glenn pulled away a tarp, dust swirling through the air. Under the tarp were several brown sacks. He took all of them outside and opened them up. One held some men's clothes. Another had a few pots, pans, matches, metal plates, and spoons and forks. The third had pillows and blankets and a few towels.

"This is all we need," Glenn declared. "I hoped it would still be here. It just needs a little airing out."

"Which way is the city?" Magnus asked. He spoke too slowly and gently, like one speaks to the very young and very old. He clutched his walking stick in his right hand and balled up his left hand into a fist.

He looked around. Everything looked the same. He peered up at the sky, and wished he knew how to read the stars, so that when they came out, they would guide him home. He considered leaving Glenn here and wandering until he found someone to help him, but with evening coming, the dread of getting lost in the dark frightened him. Magnus took a few more steps and stopped again. Neither his knee, nor body, nor his will could seem to find the energy to go onward alone.

"I'd rather not stay here," Magnus said, still speaking very slowly, his voice even and calm, as he tried a different tack. "And you're old. You deserve a nice mattress and real sheets."

"You can help build the campfire," Glenn responded.

"You cannot be my future-self. I would never choose to sleep outdoors like a homeless person."

"You'd be surprised," Glenn said, in a cheerful voice that irritated Magnus.

Magnus found and picked up two thick sticks to drum his anger out. But when he saw Elliott looking at him, he hesitated.

Then he decided to make a game of it. He gave two sticks to the boy and told him they were going to play the drums. They each hit an oak tree's trunk until their sticks fell to pieces. Sweat dripped from Magnus' forehead, and his arms felt like rubber. When he stopped, his anger and fear had passed. He dropped the two short pieces of sticks to the ground. Elliott laughed with delight at the game as he tossed the remnants of his sticks into the air over his shoulder.

Magnus decided that in the morning, he would stop at the first house they passed and phone a co-worker to pick him up. Then he would continue the search in a more civilized and logical way. He didn't care what Glenn said; he would use a map and a compass and a car to get to The Secret Bookstore.

"I'm starving," Elliott announced, rubbing his belly.

"Time to make the rabbit stew," said Glenn.

Magnus and Elliott watched in awe as Glenn prepared the stew. Like a magician, he pulled out small packages from various pockets of his shirt, pants, vest and coat. He produced salt and pepper and some basil and thyme, all of which he tossed liberally into the pot simmering over the fire. He also added the leaves, roots, mushrooms and berries he had gathered throughout the afternoon. Soon, aromatic steam wafted from the pot, and Magnus' stomach rumbled in anticipation.

When they ate, Magnus was surprised at how tasty the stew was. But he did wonder if that was only because he was so hungry from all the walking they had done that day. A leather boot soaked and cooked in water with a bit of seasoning might have been as delicious, though perhaps more difficult to chew and swallow.

"If we can't go by car, how about horse? In the movies, adventures are often taken by horse," Magnus said.

"We're in a tale, but not in the movies," Glenn said. Elliott laughed. "And none of us has a good sense of balance. We'd fall off. Truly, you've survived wealth. Sort of. Now you'll find out if you can survive poverty."

Magnus pulled out the white business card from his pocket and thought of Matilda. He looked so different than he had this morning when he'd met her after the car accident. He wondered if she would even recognize him now.

He shifted, uncomfortable in his suit pants and dress shirt. These were not the clothes he would have chosen to wear to go hiking through the countryside. After he had finished a second plate of food, he removed his dress shoes from his aching feet. Then he went into the barn and changed into the clothes Glenn had pulled out from one of the sacks. They smelt a little musty, but were dry and clean and soft against his skin. The hiking shoes fit him perfectly, and were much more comfortable than his dress shoes. The clothes would be much easier to sleep in that night. He left his ruined suit and smelly shoes in a heap in the barn. When he came back to the fire, Glenn and Elliott were gone.

A child's laugh came from the creek. Magnus glanced towards the sound, and saw Glenn walking across the water.

Walking On Water

Magnus scrambled down the hill to the creek. At the bottom of the embankment, Magnus saw that Glenn was stepping carefully from stone to stone at the shallow edge of the creek.

"I thought—," Magnus said. He let his breath out loudly.

Glenn hushed him and pointed towards Elliott. The child ran across the water, chasing a red dragonfly. Goosebumps formed on Magnus' skin. As though he sensed them staring, Elliott turned and waved.

"I almost caught that one," Elliott called out.

"Good job," Glenn said.

Elliott ran after another dragonfly.

"How is he walking on water?" Magnus whispered.

He couldn't tear his gaze away from Elliott. He was afraid to blink and miss him running.

"He's perfectly aligned with all things. He has no doubt. No one told him it was impossible, so he's not afraid of failing."

"But there are laws of nature," Magnus sputtered.

"One day you'll understand how he does it. He's fearless. Just look at him. Isn't he beautiful?" Glenn said, smiling.

Magnus watched as Elliott walked and then ran and then walked again, chasing dragonflies. The dragonflies took turns chasing each other, and then it seemed they also chased Elliott. Watching them on the creek mesmerized Magnus. He felt deep love for this child playing with dragonflies. He didn't try to stop the tears, or wipe them from his cheeks. He could not grasp it intellectually, but in his heart everything Glenn had just said made sense.

"Can you walk on water?" Magnus asked Glenn, breaking the silence.

"No. I have to use the stones." Glenn picked up a flat rock and threw it, so that it skipped across the water's surface.

"Have you ever been able to?"

"We both could, until we were boys around his age."

Magnus bent over and pushed a finger through the cold surface of the water. His injured knee quivered a little as he touched it. He was still afraid of water.

"Are you afraid of water?" Magnus asked Glenn, standing up.

"Not anymore."

"When did you stop being afraid?"

When Glenn didn't answer, Magnus turned to look at him. Glenn returned his gaze without blinking. His wrinkled face was tranquil, as Glenn said, "Around your age."

Although it grew dark, neither Glenn nor Magnus called Elliott back to shore. A wind shook the trees, causing orange and red maple leaves to whirl in the air around Elliott. He was a running silhouette against the dark blue sky, catching leaves and chasing dragonflies.

Ambushed By The Beauty Of Nature

Elliott woke up Magnus and Glenn at dawn. Magnus groaned as he sat upright. He was stiff from the car accident, from all the walking yesterday and from sleeping on the ground. The blankets Glenn had found in the barn and that they had wrapped around themselves last night were damp with dew.

"Look!" Elliott exclaimed, pointing at the sun rising over the creek.

"And look there," Glenn added, pointing to three turkey vultures sitting on a branch of a yellow and orange maple tree near the creek. They faced the sun with their wings spread out.

"What are they doing?" Elliott asked.

"Their body temperature drops at night. They're slightly hypothermic now, and before they can fly they need the sun to warm them up. And the sun will dry dew off of their wings." Glenn threw off his damp blanket and stood up. "If they have bacteria on them from the dead animals they've eaten, the sun disinfects that too."

"Cool," Elliott said.

"All these quiet moments of preparation makes their flight look easy," Glenn said.

Magnus pulled out his leather journal and scribbled down everything Glenn had just told them.

"I still think they're ugly," he muttered, wrapping the blanket around his shoulders.

"I think they're beautiful!" Elliott exclaimed. "Can I go to the creek and look closer?"

"No," said Magnus at the same time that Glenn said, "Yes."

With wide, pleading eyes, Elliott looked from Glenn to Magnus.

"I've heard of vultures attacking cats and dogs," Magnus said in a low voice, looking at Glenn. "Even small goats and sheep."

"That's a myth born of fear. I've never seen it with my own eyes," Glenn said.

"Please," Elliott begged.

"The birds won't grab him?" Magnus asked.

An owl hooted. At the sudden sound, Magnus jerked, his blanket falling to the ground.

"Consider that everyone thinks that owls are so wise," Glenn said. "But did you know they will kill other birds—their own kind? Do you know how dangerous they are?"

"Really?" Elliott asked.

"Ah, not to you," Glenn said. "But dangerous to other birds. In contrast the vultures' talons are blunt and their beaks are too weak to kill. They clean up the mess no one else wants to face. And they care for their own kind, making sure they call other vultures to come and share a feast. Who has the greater wisdom?"

"I'd rather that owls were following us than vultures," Magnus said, firmly.

"You'd rather be followed by murderers?" Glenn asked.

"You have a funny way of twisting things," Magnus said, crossing his arms over his chest.

"*Catharses Aura* is the Latin name of the turkey vulture. It means 'golden purifier' or 'purifying breeze.' You understand, Elliott? They clean up the world for us."

"Like a vacuum?" Elliott asked.

"Sort of like turning compost into a garden," Glenn said.

"I know the vultures aren't murderers," Elliott said, confidently. "Can I go look closer now? Please?"

Magnus glanced at Glenn and then reluctantly said, "All right."

With a shout of joy and triumph, Elliott scampered off.

"The vultures are watching out for us, truly," Glenn said. "Look there."

Magnus turned to join him in watching the pink rising sun. The beauty that had appeared in the sky while they had been talking surprised him. As crickets chirped, cicadas sang from the trees and frogs gulped from the creek's edge, Magnus watched the sun, now and then glancing at Glenn, who stared at it enraptured as if it were a theatrical performance.

Shaking his head in awe, Glenn said, "The beauty of nature ambushes us."

"It's an assault on the senses." Magnus rubbed his tired eyes. "I feel like I should put on full armour and a helmet with a visor and take up a sword to protect myself."

In his leather book Magnus scribbled down a few phrases about the sun and armour.

"Once you get used to seeing nature without a filter, it won't feel like an assault anymore," Glenn said. "It will feel less like a sword fight and more like a dance, in which you partner with the beauty. But nature will always take the lead. You must remember that. If you try to lead, it will turn into a fight again."

"Are you a poet?" Magnus asked.

"I observe, but don't write things down. I leave that to you."

At the creek, as he listened to the men talk, Elliott poked a stick where the sun's pink reflection broke in fragments across the water. Magnus watched closely, hoping Elliott would run across the water again like the night before.

"Once, when I was a boy his age, I thought I could capture the sun glowing in a river," Glenn said. "I leaned over to grab it."

Elliott dropped his stick and bent over and put his hand

into the water.

"And?" Magnus asked.

"All I felt was water," Glenn continued.

"I looked right at the sun and I didn't go blind!" Elliott shouted up at the men.

"That's what I thought too," Glenn murmured.

Magnus did not understand the deeper meaning behind Glenn and Elliott's words, but sensed there was one. He scribbled the story about the sun's reflection in his leather journal as well.

As one of the vultures stood up and shifted on the branch, Magnus noticed it had white streaks on its legs. As though he had heard Magnus' thoughts, Elliott asked: "Why does it have white on its legs?" He came back to the campsite and the fire that Glenn had ignited from last night's embers. "Is it sick?"

"They defecate on their own legs," Glenn said. "It cleans them of bacteria and in the summer cools them down. And, to scare away predators, they vomit on them. That's their weapon."

"Wow. That's cool," Elliott said.

"Much, much more than I needed to know," Magnus said with a grimace.

But although he tried to look away, his eyes remained glued to the birds, who continued to face the rising pink disk of the sun.

Sharing Fear

As twigs and branches burned briskly, Glenn boiled sorrel roots that he had dug up yesterday. Nearby Elliott caught black crickets and grasshoppers. Once Elliott decided that he had caught enough of each, Glenn fried the insects over the fire. Even though Glenn insisted that the crickets were full of nutritious protein and would taste delicious with the salt he sprinkled on, Magnus refused to try them. Instead he ate the sorrel roots, that tasted like potatoes, sprinkled with salt and pepper.

When they had finished eating, Elliott gathered wild grapes in his shiny birthday hat and passed them to Glenn and Magnus for dessert. Magnus would have preferred a chocolate croissant and hot coffee, but when he saw how much fun Elliott had helping prepare breakfast, he found himself enjoying the food.

After savouring the last grape, Magnus put on the hiking shoes he had taken from the barn the previous evening, and, with Elliott, went down to the creek. Magnus' heart pounded and he broke into a cold sweat as he looked at the water's smooth surface and took the boy's small hand in his. Glenn watched as they both stepped out onto the water.

Magnus heard the faintest whisper: *Coward.*

He disregarded the voice, ignored the pain slicing through his knee and continued stepping forward. But instead of Magnus walking on water, Elliott sank with Magnus.

Magnus insisted on taking several more strides. Each of their steps plunged through the water, their feet touching the gravel bottom. Elliott shivered at the feel of the cold water seeping into his shoes. They returned to shore with wet feet and pants. Elliott ran back to the campfire to dry and warm himself.

Glenn joined Magnus at the creek's edge.

"Why did he sink?" Magnus asked Glenn, trying to hide his deep disappointment. He pulled off his wet shoes and socks and shook them so vigorously drops of water flew around them.

"You shared your fears with him," Glenn answered.

At the edge of the water, a turtle, covered with green moss and the size of a dinner plate, moved. Magnus stepped towards it, thinking he would catch it for Elliott. Glenn pulled him back, just as the turtle opened its mouth and snapped at Magnus' walking stick. Magnus yanked it back, but the turtle held onto it with its powerful jaws.

"You almost lost a finger there," Glenn said. "That's a

snapping turtle you tried to pick up."

Together the two men managed to yank the walking stick away from the turtle. However, the animal left deep indents in the bottom of the stick from its bite.

"Can Elliott teach me to be fearless?" Magnus asked.

Glenn didn't answer. Instead he stroked his beard, as he so often did. Magnus touched his own cheeks and chin, which now had a day's growth of hair.

"I want to be fearless," Magnus said. When he heard the words aloud, he was surprised at himself. But he also understood they were true and felt the depth of his desire. "It has to be possible again, right? I could become like Elliott again?"

"I'll bring you to the forest, and we'll keep looking for the bookstore," Glenn answered.

Later that morning they came across a pond.

"Let's catch one," Elliott said, pointing at a skating water bug.

Magnus took Elliott's hand. Ignoring his thumping heart, Magnus told himself he had to try again. Together they stepped out onto the pond. He was deeply disappointed when both his and Elliott's feet sank through the water's surface. Magnus wanted to continue walking, but when he stepped forward, Elliott refused to move.

"Maybe your friend Robin can help you," Magnus suggested.

Elliott shook his head so hard that his birthday hat fell off.

The rest of that day, whenever they came across a pond or ditch or puddle, Elliott would go near it to throw in sticks or stones, or to look for turtles or frogs. He'd poke at the mud at the edges, but he refused to step out onto any body of water again with Magnus.

They stopped walking late in the afternoon by another creek. Glenn and Elliott sat under a weeping willow, and fished with rods Glenn made from tree branches and fish hooks he had in his coat pocket.

Several feet away from them, Magnus stepped out on the water. Before plunging his foot completely into the water and getting wet socks and shoes again, he pulled it back. His shoulders slumped.

Elliott cheered, as he pulled up the hook and line Glenn had made. A small silver fish flopped on the end.

The boy thanked his invisible friend for helping him catch the fish, while Magnus forced himself to smile.

"I believe that Elliott won't be able to walk on water again," Glenn said. He tugged the end of his beard. Then he let it go, so it rested against his chest.

He sat with Magnus at the evening campfire, near an

abandoned cabin that had provided a frying pan and a few dishes and cutlery and cups. He cooked the six fish that he and Elliott had caught that afternoon.

"Why didn't you stop me from first trying to walk out on the water with Elliott? Did you know what would happen?" Magnus asked. The chill evening air penetrated his jacket. He shivered and moved closer to the fire to warm himself.

"I'm not surprised," Glenn said. He turned the fish over, cooking them evenly on each side. "But I don't know your future."

"You should have stopped me," Magnus said. He crossed his arms in front of him and glared at Glenn.

"Instead, I gave you a gift. Now you'll keep searching for the bookstore. If you found the way to walk on water now, you might return home to your job, without getting the book you seek."

Magnus gritted his teeth and grumbled to himself.

"Proper timing. Proper times," Glenn said. He stroked his beard again, tugging the end of it. His cheerful demeanor irritated Magnus.

"I thought there was no such thing as time," Magnus pointed out.

"True enough," Glenn said. "So no need for us to hurry. Truly, no need in life to hurry."

"Have you been looking for the bookstore all these years?" Magnus uncrossed his arms and shuffled his feet. "Don't you want to hurry up and find it?"

"I know my purpose. I don't need to look for anything. I just take note of whatever I see."

Magnus sighed, as Glenn laughed.

Words Both Indecipherable And Familiar

Later that evening, while sitting at the campfire, Glenn took out a book from his canvas sack. It had no cover. He flipped through it, and ripped out several pages.

Magnus gasped and said, "Books are sacred objects!"

"The cover was already missing," Glenn said. "It's at my house. Once we get there, we'll lay all the pieces out side by side and it will make a new whole."

Magnus had read all the time as a boy, but as an adult he had become too busy to read. He wondered now if he had busied himself to deal with the emptiness in his life because he had stopped reading.

Elliott and Magnus each took several pages. When Magnus looked at the words, he found they were both indecipherable and familiar. Elliott traced his finger over the letters.

"These are like your tattoos," Elliott exclaimed.

As soon as he said this, Magnus saw that the words on the page were identical to the markings on Glenn's arms.

"What do they mean?" Magnus asked. He imitated Elliott, tracing his own figure over the shapes of the marks on the page.

"It's the language of the trees," Glenn said. "But its secrets haven't been entirely revealed to me."

"Do the trees talk?" Elliott asked.

"Always," Glenn said, as Magnus said, "No."

Magnus peered more closely at the symbols and like Elliott traced several with a fingertip. The markings looked like something elves might write.

"Magnus, I hoped you might translate it for me," Glenn said. "It's visual poetry. I thought you might understand it. I'm willing to learn from you too."

Magnus was surprised that Glenn had such faith in him. He felt like he had as a young child, when he first looked in awe at letters in a book. Even before he knew what the letters and words meant, it felt like they silently communicated to him just by existing. He peeked at Elliott, whose face was shining with delight as he studied the symbols.

Nearby trees creaked and moaned as their branches rubbed against each other. Magnus and Elliott glanced up at the rustling leaves.

"They're talking," Elliott said with a grin.

"Could be," Magnus and Glenn both said.

The evening sky was so spacious it overwhelmed Magnus. To take it all in, he felt that he had to break it down by looking at it through the branches and leaves of the trees and seeing just patches of it. As he studied it this way, coyotes yipped and yapped in the distance.

"They're talking too," Elliott said, nestling into the blankets and pillows that Glenn had taken from the cabin.

"I wish I understood it all," Magnus said.

"Not me," said Elliott. "I like just listening."

"Me too," Glenn said.

All three of them settled down and fell asleep for the night as the trees and animals spoke around them, the pages of the ripped book tucked under their pillows.

The Man In White

"Here we are," Glenn announced. He pointed with his walking stick to the edge of a forest. "My home."

Magnus studied the flaming autumn leaves. The trees were beautiful, but looked no different than other forests they had passed during their last five days of walking together.

"I share my home with our friends, the turkey vultures. They roost here at the edge of the forest." Glenn waved his stick vaguely at the trees.

Magnus peered at the forest, unable to see any of the birds.

"Truly, they're there," Glenn said. "Generations of vultures have slept here, for at least a hundred years. They've spent a lifetime watching over us."

"Wow," Elliott said, peering into the shadows of the forest's edge. "How long is a lifetime?"

"Very long. Do you think the roosting place is their destination or starting point?" Glenn asked them.

Magnus and Elliott answered simultaneously.

"Destination," Magnus said.

"The start," Elliott said.

"One journey ends," Glenn said, with a shrug. "Another begins."

"The bookstore is here, right?" Magnus asked. "It's not much farther, is it? Isn't this where we've been headed towards?"

A distant voice interrupted their conversation. "Hellooooo!"

A man walked towards them from the treeline. He wore a white suit, white tie and white dress shoes, and swung a white briefcase. His hair was also white, glowing in the sun. The man waved them forward. When they had neared, Magnus saw that his face was deeply tanned and had the texture of leather. The man said in a gravelly voice: "Don't go in there."

"Why not?" Elliott asked, now looking with some nervousness at the forest.

"People waste their entire lives wandering around in there, looking for a bookstore that doesn't exist."

"How do you know it doesn't exist?" Magnus asked. All his doubts about the journey bubbled up from where he had pushed them away.

"I've never seen it." The man in white lifted his chin in the air.

"Have you seen Paris?" Glenn asked.

"No." The man sniffed loudly. "Never."

"Does it exist?" Glenn responded.

"Of course."

"But you haven't seen it. So how can you know?" Magnus crossed his arms over his chest.

"I won't be tricked with these childish games and riddles," the man said, his voice rising to a half-shout. "I haven't seen one person come out this way with a book."

He dropped his briefcase to the grass, revealing its black underside. Having noticed the strange colouring of the briefcase, Magnus looked more closely at the man. Now he saw that there were black patches on the suit under his arms. He could just see a ridge of black at the bottom edges of the man's shoes. The man's suit, shoes and briefcase had all once been entirely black, but the sun had faded them to white.

"Maybe they leave by a different way," Magnus suggested, his gaze flickering from the man's shoes to his bronzed face, as he inched backwards.

Glenn stroked his beard, and then he scratched his head, as though thinking deeply about this possibility.

"Robin says that you're not wrong," Elliott said to Magnus.

"Then it must be true," Glenn said.

Because Magnus felt a growing distrust of the man in white, he took Elliott's hand in his own to keep him near and safe. Elliott pulled his shiny blue birthday hat low over his eyes, as he did when shy or nervous.

"In there is the darkest forest," the man in white said, his voice rising into a bellow, like a preacher on a pulpit, determined to persuade his congregation of some deep truth. "You'll spend weeks or years or the rest of your life wandering around. Come with me and walk towards the sun."

He picked the briefcase up and stabbed the air with it like it was a sword, pointing it up towards the sun.

"Is that what you do?" Magnus said, narrowing his eyes as he continued to study the man's tanned skin and white clothes.

"Yes. All day," the man said, nodding slowly and pompously. He lowered the briefcase and swung it from side to side.

"Then you don't get far," Magnus said. "You head east and then west. You stand still at noon. You end at nearly the same spot every day."

"I don't go far, but I know where I'm going," the man in white retorted. "I'm always in the brightest light. And all along this stretch, I warn people about the darkness of the forest."

Again the man vigorously swung his briefcase around him. Magnus backed away and turned to Glenn.

"How far to your house?" Magnus asked Glenn.

"Three days walking," Glenn said. "The forest is very large. And I live in the heart of it."

Magnus let go of Elliott's hand, shocked to learn that that the journey wasn't nearly over. He had assumed once they arrived at the forest, they would be at Glenn's house. Throughout the trip, Glenn had only spoke of coming to the forest, not the journey into the forest once they got here.

"I'm going to look for grasshoppers," Elliott interrupted, running off to the edge of the forest.

Magnus sat down on a large rock. He felt weary. The days of walking had exhausted him. The thought of more walking made him feel even more fatigued. He rested his chin in his hands, his elbows on his knees.

Glenn sat beside him. The sun-bleached man walked away from them towards the east, where the sun shone brightly in the September sky.

Magnus considered the words of the man in the white suit. The thought of spending his entire life wandering through a dark forest looking for a bookstore that might or might not exist frightened him. He could still return to his old life. While just days ago he had thought he would never return to the city until he had found the bookstore, now he doubted his own resolve and courage. He lowered his head, ashamed of his cowardice.

"It's not the darkness of the forest that will destroy this man in white," Glenn said, placing his walking stick across his knees. "He will be destroyed by his fear of the dark. This man has wasted his day. He's wasted this moment standing here warning people, instead of living his life."

"I don't want to waste my life," Magnus mumbled, his eyes still downcast. He brushed his fingers over the soft moss on the rock, and shifted his feet and legs. He felt edgy, but was unsure if the feeling meant he was restless to go onward or to go home or if he was just afraid. He glanced up at the sun-bleached man walking away from them, and then dropped his eyes back to the ground.

"He's the type who moves constantly and goes nowhere," Glenn said. "Because he is afraid, he wants everyone in the entire world to be afraid with him. Because he will not try, he wants no one else to try. In trying to avoid fear, he creates more fear."

Magnus pressed his hand against his eyelid, which had begun to twitch. He touched the moss again with his other hand, noting that it was both soft and hard beneath the softness. That was how he wanted to be: soft and gentle, but strong and firm beneath—like Glenn.

As his gaze moved across the edge of the forest, suddenly, Magnus saw three turkey vultures standing up and shifting in place on the branch of a maple tree. He realized that they had been there all along, and were just now coming into his awareness. With awkwardness they stood, and shifted in place. Then they hopped, and flapped their wings, finally rising from the tree into the air.

Magnus took out his leather book and scribbled down a few lines, describing the way the birds left the tree branch. As he was writing, he realized the birds' clumsy awkwardness, moving from standing to flight, was this exact moment he was now in—the moment of transition, leaving this place of sunlight on a warm rock, for the darkness of the forest. If he moved onward, he might look as graceless.

He also understood that in attempting to only follow the sun, this man in white was trying to remain within the illusion of constant safety. Magnus looked at Elliott crouched near some Queen's Anne's lace, looking for grasshoppers, and decided he wanted to teach Elliott fearlessness—to let the boy live fully like every day was a birthday celebration.

"I trust you," Magnus said to Glenn. "Safe or dangerous, dark or light, let's go on."

The men stood up, leaning on their walking sticks.

"True enough, most of the forest light is filtered," Glenn said, patting Magnus' back. "But surely the shadows are just shade. We don't need to be frightened of them."

Magnus hoped Glenn was right, as again he saw the now-familiar shadowy figure disappearing into the edge of the forest and heard a soft whisper: *Coward.* A sharp pain sliced through his knee.

The Firefighters

Glenn walked along the forest until he saw a large snake curled up on a branch.

"Here's the entrance," he said.

As Elliott admired the green snake, Glenn pulled aside vines and shrubs, and entered the forest. Magnus and Elliott followed, branches and twigs scratching their arms.

Magnus looked behind him; the vines and branches had already fallen back into place, and completely hidden the place where they had entered. The snake was no longer visible.

As Glenn led them forward, the forest became less dense; filtered light trickled through tree tops and danced around their feet. Magnus looked back once again, realizing with some anxiety that he'd never find his own way out. If Elliott ran ahead and disappeared, they might never find him again, Magnus realized, his shoulders tightening at the thought.

Studying the forest, Magnus nervously tapped his fingers on his walking stick. Trees, branches, underbrush, roots and logs were all scattered without any seeming order. It felt chaotic. There were no paths or trails, like one might find in a park or campground. The forest was nothing like the city, with its carefully angled streets and ordered houses and buildings.

"Welcome to the Garden of Eden," Glenn said, gesturing around them.

"This?" Magnus exclaimed.

"Garden of eatin'?" Elliott asked. "Yummy. Are there chocolate bars here?"

Both men laughed, and Magnus instantly felt less afraid as he listened to their laughter bounce off the tree tops and echo around them.

"I wouldn't mind a chocolate bar myself." Magnus' mouth watered at the thought.

"In the forest everything is always changing, but always the same," Glenn said. "Always new and always familiar. Truly, there is no imperfection in the forest. Every tree, crooked or straight, tall or stunted, dying or growing, is exactly as it is meant to be."

"Where did those come from?" Elliott asked, pointing at several trees to their immediate right that were so enormous their trunks were big enough to allow a car to drive through.

Magnus joined Elliott in leaning back to look up to the tree tops.

"This section of the forest is ancient," Glenn said. "These large trees have existed since the creation of time. They've always been here."

Magnus believed Glenn, for the forest had a sense of eternity about it. The only sounds were distant birds and the occasional whirring of flies. Beneath those sounds there was a nearly tangible hush.

"How many years have you lived in the forest?" Magnus asked.

"Fifty," Glenn said. "Give or take a year or two. I've regretted none of them. Before I moved here, in my youth, I traveled the entire world. But I have found no better place to live my life than the forest."

This intrigued Magnus for throughout the journey Glenn had continually refused to answer questions about his past, even though Magnus had repeatedly tried to get some scraps of information from him.

"You never were an accountant, were you?" Magnus asked. "Does that mean I'll travel the world too?"

"You don't seem like the type to look for adventure," Glenn said. "Truly, I suspect I might have done all the traveling you'll need to do."

Magnus touched one of the enormous tree trunks with his finger tips. The wood felt warm and, in a way he couldn't explain, gentle and comforting to the touch, like it was alive and touching him back.

Ahead of them a crow flitted from a tree to the forest floor, across dried pine needles and leaves.

"The crow wants to tell us something!" Elliott declared. His eyes shone at the prospect of a new adventure.

"Is it a sign?" Magnus asked. He felt hopeful, wanting the bird to mean something.

Elliott leaned down and stepped towards the crow. It darted away from them to the top of a rusty 1960s fire truck partially hidden by tangled brush and undergrowth. Elliott ran ahead to investigate. He tripped over some invisible twig or rock, and then pulled himself upright just before falling. Magnus and Glenn followed him.

"Is the fire coming?" a man cried, as the three of them neared. His dark brown eyes darted around wildly.

A man and a woman in their fifties, each wearing a firefighter's uniform, held a hose. They shot water from the hose into the air above Elliott. Several drops of water splattered on them. Elliott wiped his forehead, as Magnus leapt in front of the boy to shield him in case the firefighters blasted water again.

"What fire?" Magnus asked, not seeing flames or smoke anywhere. He looked around quickly, afraid he was missing something.

"The fire that's coming," the man said.

They sprayed more water, this time hitting a black walnut tree above them, causing golden leaves to scatter. Several of the tennis-ball-sized walnuts fell and hit Magnus on the head. Elliott giggled and adjusted his birthday hat, as though it would protect him from falling nuts. The light lime smell of the walnuts wafted upwards and around them.

"There's no fire," Elliott said innocently, from behind Magnus. "Just a crow."

"Do you mean the fire isn't here yet?" the female firefighter asked.

Both firefighters looked disappointed. The man relaxed, dropped the hose and leaned against the truck. He removed his helmet. His damp black hair stuck up in wild tufts. The woman remained standing, holding the hose with her hands.

"How long have you been here?" Magnus asked.

"It feels like forever," the fireman said, sighing.

"That long?" Elliott asked with wide eyes. He peeked from behind Magnus to see if it was safe.

"You could just go home and enjoy life," Glenn said, more gently than Magnus had ever heard him speak before.

The woman also removed her helmet and set the hose down. Elliott slipped between Glenn and Magnus and took their hands in each of his. Magnus suddenly felt intensely protective of the boy, and moved closer to guard him, if needed.

"Maybe we could do that," she said, looking hopefully at the man. She removed her heavy gloves. "I've always wanted to plant a rose garden. They're my favourite flower."

"If we wait here long enough, a fire will come. And when it

does, we have to be ready," the man said, his voice stern and confident.

"Do you like wearing the uniforms all the time?" Elliott asked.

Instead of answering, the woman held out her fire hat for him to try on. He took off his misshapen and mud-stained birthday hat and handed it to Glenn. The fire hat covered half of Elliott's face, so Glenn helped pull it back so he could see. The couple then showed Elliott the inside of the truck and let him try to lift the hose. He pushed a button that once had caused a siren to sound. It squeaked. Elliott frowned in disappointment at the sound.

"Can I go for a ride?" Elliott asked. "Please?"

"No tires," the man said, pointing at the truck, where the tires had deflated and fallen away in large strips.

"Then how will you get to the fire?" Elliott asked, wrinkling his snub nose.

"It will come to us, of course," the woman said, picking up the hose again. "That's why we're waiting."

"Do you want the fire to come?" Elliott asked.

Magnus wondered the same thing, feeling there was something wrong with these people. He shifted uneasily in place.

"No, but we have to be ready when it does. We want to feel safe. If we aren't prepared, we'll be taken by surprise."

"You don't like surprises?" Elliott asked. He tilted his head to the side, as though he couldn't fathom anyone who didn't like a surprise. He removed the fire hat and put on the birthday hat again. His demeanor brightened. "Robin and I love surprises."

"But if the fire never comes, won't you have wasted your time here?" Magnus asked.

Glenn interrupted the conversation to say they had to continue on their journey. Magnus agreed, relieved to be leaving the waiting firefighters.

"I'm sorry you can't come to find treasures with us," Elliott said. "Snakes and rocks and acorns and—."

"We're doing important work here," the woman said firmly. "When you're older, you'll understand."

"You can have one of my treasures. Which one do you want?" Elliott peered into the pail. "Oh, the cricket I caught jumped out."

At his look of distress, Glenn assured him that they could find other crickets, as well as grasshoppers and praying mantises. This cheered the boy. He gave each of the firefighters one black and orange caterpillar from his pail.

"The black stripes on a caterpillar tell us about the coming winter," Glenn said. "Lots of black at the front means an early snowfall and hard start to winter. Lots of black at the end of the caterpillar means a hard end to winter. If the black stripes are small, the winter will be easy."

The five of them studied the crawling caterpillar that the

man held in his hand. The orange in the middle was a small stripe. Most of the caterpillar was black at the front and back end. Then they studied the second caterpillar sitting still in the woman's hand. This one also only had a narrow orange band.

"A hard winter then," the male firefighter said. He stuck the helmet back on his head and his dark eyes darted around the forest again. "Be prepared."

In answer Elliott picked up a walnut, tossed it in his pail and ran ahead of them.

"Magnus, don't worry. You will be ready for the winter," Glenn said. "I'll see to it."

"What? Won't I be home by then?" Magnus asked, shocked.

"Not likely," Glenn said. "But then I don't remember exactly how things go. I'm getting older. And you have your own path to take."

"I know. I know. My own choices. My journey. The future is flexible."

"Flexible and fluid as water," Glenn said.

"I'm going to choose a quick and easy and short journey to the bookstore," Magnus declared.

In response, Glenn laughed, the sound echoing off the tree tops. Magnus doubted his own words.

Glenn's Home

In the late afternoon of the third day of walking through the forest, they reached a clearing where Glenn's house stood. Wide beams of sunlight penetrated through the tree tops and lit the area. His home consisted of a group of lopsided buildings connected by enclosed walkways. A tree grew up through the centre of one building. Or, perhaps, Magnus thought, the building had been built around the tree. Several floors had been built in the arms of an oak tree. The grey, weathered boards had been haphazardly hammered together, so the walls all leaned at odd angles, just like the crooked tree branches and trunks.

Glenn had settled into the forest as unobtrusively as possible, and, it seemed, the forest aimed to reclaim the buildings; oak leaves gathered in the corner of the entranceway and needles from nearby pine trees piled at the edges of the house. Leaves and twigs littered the corners of the roof.

"The house was here when I came," Glenn said. "I just

took it over and maintained it."

They entered the house through a heavy oak door. A chipmunk greeted them by scrambling around the back entrance way, and then darting between their feet and outside. Glenn led Magnus through the hall into the kitchen, as Elliott ran ahead to explore. Magnus dropped his journal and jacket onto the kitchen table and followed Elliott through the house. Spider webs had accumulated in corners of most of the rooms, and Elliott struck down the webs that he could reach with his arms and hands. In a corner of the living room, Elliott found and caught a brown snake, and at Magnus' insistence, put it outside. Moments later, he ran back in to join the men.

The back of the house had a living room that Glenn had turned into a sort of natural museum. Bookshelves lined the walls, and about fifty books adorned them. Glenn had filled the areas of the shelves that did not hold books with pine cones, stones, leaves, bird feathers and the skeletons of small animals—the treasures of a young boy or a naturalist. The animal bones immediately attracted the interest of Elliott, who studied the skull of a squirrel.

As he looked at the shelves of books and natural objects Magnus had an intense desire to write a poem.

"Here," Glenn said, passing Magnus a book from the shelf. "Just write the poem in the front or back cover."

"I don't want to ruin your book. And how did you know?"

Glenn shrugged, with a wide grin, and then said: "It's all just added value. I'd be honoured if you wrote it in there."

Magnus took the book and pen and wrote:

Meeting Place

I am

quieter here
in the forest I am

quieter, hear

the forest

Magnus replaced the book on the shelf. On a nearby shelf, Glenn had laid out the parts of a book like they were a skeleton—the spine, the front and back cover and loose pages. Another shelf held the various pieces of a clock. They both looked like someone had performed an autopsy on them.

"Look closely," Glenn said. "Things are no longer what they were, when they come apart and you see components. But each piece might be more complete than the whole."

From his canvas sack, Glenn removed the coverless book with the mysterious hieroglyphics. He also took out the loose pages that he had ripped from it. Then he picked up a red cover that was lying on the lowest shelf and placed the book beside it, so the various pieces of it were visible and displayed in a group.

Elliott slipped up beside them and picked up a coil that had come from the clock and threw it into his pail, promising to make something from it later. He tossed his crumpled hat on the shelf where the coil had been.

"To him, that coil is more interesting and important than an intact working clock," Glenn said.

Magnus agreed, as he nearly tripped over a pile of newspapers. Something about the house reminded him a little of his condo. He had various piles of intentions—books he planned to read, newspapers he had skimmed over and wanted to recycle, groceries that needed to be put away and laundry to sort. It looked disorganized to an outsider, but to the owner the system was perfectly logical.

The sound of pattering above them caused both Magnus and Elliott to freeze. Glenn broke into a grin.

"Squirrels," Glenn said. "They're gathering pine cones and nuts. They run from tree to tree across the roof. I've quite grown to like them—rather like erratic raindrops."

"Better outside than in," Magnus said, wryly.

"Oh, they try to get inside too," Glenn said. "More than once I've woken in the night to a squirrel dashing across my bed."

Magnus shivered.

"That's friendly of them to visit," Elliott said. "Can I keep one as a pet?"

"The pet grasshopper is probably enough," Magnus said, glaring at Glenn.

"If you can catch the squirrel, you can keep it," Glenn said.

Elliott accepted the answer as a challenge and raced outside to chase a squirrel.

The Good Witch

A person moved amongst the trees. Glenn grabbed Elliott's hand, and told him to be still. Magnus' heart thumped loudly, afraid it was the shadowy figure who seemed to be stalking him.

Both of the men relaxed again as an elderly woman with scraggly white hair walked out from between two oaks. She strode purposefully towards them. Because of her age Magnus felt he should run to her and offer her an arm to lean on, or give her his walking stick. But a straightness to her shoulders and a confidence about her suggested that she needed no help, even if she moved slowly.

"It's the Good Witch," Glenn said, releasing Elliott's hand.

"Can witches be good?" Elliott asked the invisible being beside him.

Glenn patted Elliott's shoulder. "Her real name is Amelia. She's just an old woman with eccentricities and a lot of determination and a sharp tongue."

"Then why is she called The Good Witch?" Elliott asked,

his brow furrowed.

"She's strongminded and peculiar and straight-forward. The name suited her. She calls herself that to scare away the cowardly people who come here. She owns this forest. I work for her as the forest warden."

Amelia wore layers of brown and green dresses, skirts and shirts. They were covered with patches and loose pieces of material, making her look like a large, wild bird. Perched on her shoulder, an enormous raven ruffled its feathers. The black bird was so large it stood a few inches above her head. Magnus guessed it was the size of a large parrot, perhaps twenty-five inches long from tail to the tip of its beak.

"A trespasser has cut down two trees," Amelia announced to Glenn, when she was within speaking distance. She looked at Elliott and Magnus with fierce dark eyes that were as lovely and dangerous as glass flowers. "Who are they?"

"I'm here to find The Secret Bookstore," Magnus said, and showed her the business card he kept in his pocket.

She was tiny, hardly over four feet, so Magnus could see the top of her head; the pink of her scalp was visible through thin white wisps of hair. She barely glanced at the card, and then she murmured something indecipherable as she turned to Glenn and asked: "Is it them?"

"Yes."

"So soon. Time moves quickly."

She rapidly blinked her eyes. Glenn patted her arm.

Immediately, in response, the raven lunged towards Glenn. Glenn didn't flinch, but Magnus jumped backwards in surprise, his eyes glued to the bird's large knife-like black beak.

"I've seen your tricks before," Glenn said to the bird.

The raven settled again on Amelia's shoulder, where it made a low guttural noise. Amelia smoothed the shaggy feathers at its throat.

"How old are you?" Elliott asked Amelia.

"I'm a hundred and thirty years old," she said.

Her deeply wrinkled face suggested she might be close to that age. But although her hands and face were covered with brown age spots, her eyes had the life and sharpness of a young woman.

"That's very old," Elliott announced, nodding sagely.

"Old enough," she said, nonchalantly. She continued stroking the bird with her gnarled fingers.

"Does the bird talk?" Elliott asked.

"He spoke once," Amelia said. "But then he realized that he had said all he needed to say. Now he's silent."

Magnus was about to laugh, but stopped at her serious expression. She stopped stroking the raven's neck and touched its large beak.

"What's his name?" Elliott asked. He set down his pail and reached out to pet the bird, thought better of it, and picked up his pail again.

"Raven," Amelia said. She took her fingers from the bird,

pointed at Magnus and Elliott, turned to Glenn, and asked: "Are we taking them with us?"

"Magnus will want to learn more about the forest, and Elliott can't be left here alone."

"I'll look for the bookstore as we go," Magnus said. "Unless you're the owner?"

Amelia cackled then, just as a witch would. "Why do you want to find this—this— store?"

"A woman with red hair, Matilda, gave me this card and said I would find a book there that could tell me my life purpose. I want to walk on water. I want to be fearless," Magnus said, his voice fading under her sharp, judging gaze.

He looked down at his feet, feeling like he was withering under her eyes. He felt cowardly to be intimidated by such an elderly woman.

"One of those people—looking for their purpose and the meaning of life," she said, and cackled again.

The raven gave one long grating caw. To Magnus it sounded as though the bird said, *Fool.* Its beady black eyes looked at him intensely, with an intelligence that Magnus had observed in the eyes of smart dogs, but never a bird. He made a note to himself not to trust the creature.

Cut-Down Trees

Amelia led them to a dense part of the forest. Magnus noted that here, while there were many trees, some very large, none were as enormous as those few ancient ones they saw when they first entered the forest three days ago.

She showed them the place where the trespasser had sawed down the trees. The first one had been a maple tree in full leaf, but it was hollow inside.

"Was it dead?" Elliott asked.

He pulled out a chunk of rotted wood, and dropped it into his pail. Then he picked up a handful of sawdust from the ground and threw it upward. It scattered and some landed on Amelia's brown leather boots. In response she glared at the boy, her eyes like glowing coals. The raven sat on a branch above them, and swivelled its head from Elliott to Amelia, and back to the child, its shiny eyes missing nothing. Elliott ignored Amelia and the raven and picked up another handful of sawdust. This time, though, he moved aside before he threw it upward, so it wouldn't land on her.

"It was sick inside," Amelia said. "No one could have known until it was cut down that it was rotten to the core. It could have fallen at any time."

There was a note nailed to the fallen tree. It said: *I'm looking for the bookstore. I know it's hidden in a tree and how would I know if it's hollow or not, unless I cut it down?*

A second tree, without any leaves on it, had also been cut down.

"Was this one dead?" Elliott asked.

"It was alive," Amelia said. "The leaves fell off early."

Amelia showed them the note that had been nailed to this tree. Magnus read aloud: "*There's too much darkness in the forest. I'm trying to let in the light.*"

"How much light do we need in the forest?" Elliott asked.

"At the appropriate, places the sun reaches the forest floor," Glenn said, tapping his walking stick on the ground with each word. "No need to cut down trees."

The raven left the branch, and flew in loops in the space above them. It had more space to fly now since the two trees had been cut down and several smaller trees had been crushed by the fall of the larger ones. Elliott marvelled at raven's skills, and the length of its black wings, while Glenn ignored the bird, and stroked his beard several times. He then studied the ground around the area for human tracks. Although he felt inadequate in his tracking skills, Magnus was determined to help and looked around with Glenn look for any clues. Neither of them saw any evidence of the intruder.

"There is a reason the bookstore is hidden," Amelia said to Magnus, as the bird returned to sit on her shoulder.

"Why?" Magnus asked, leaning towards her.

She glared at him without answering for a long moment. He looked back as long as he could, before dropping his gaze to his hiking shoes.

Then she said, "I would think it's obvious."

"Of course, it *is* obvious," Magnus stuttered. His eyes remained on his feet. He shuffled in place. "Yes. Very obvious."

"And the reason?"

Magnus opened and closed his mouth, but no words came out. He was afraid of saying the wrong thing. He glanced up at her.

"Few are worthy of finding it," Amelia said.

"That's the truth," Glenn said.

"Of course. I understand. And someone who would cut down beautiful healthy trees shouldn't ever get a book and—." Magnus stopped speaking, for Amelia turned her back on him and was clearly not interested in his fumbling explanation.

Amelia started walking back towards Glenn's house. Glenn followed, catching up to her with several long strides. The raven flew ahead of them.

"I will find the trespasser cutting down the trees," Glenn

promised Amelia.

Again he touched her arm. As Magnus noted the tenderness in his action, he understood that Glenn cared deeply for Amelia. But because she was so acerbic, he could not tell if Amelia returned his feelings. However, he wondered, if just allowing Glenn to touch her, revealed that she cared for him too.

Chopping Wood

Back at his house, Glenn asked Magnus to gather and then chop fallen branches. Magnus would have preferred to help Glenn look for the person cutting down the trees, and search for the bookstore at the same time, but Glenn insisted that Magnus had the most important job, explaining that they needed wood to heat the house through the winter. Glenn decided to take Elliott along with him to continue to teach him how to track animals.

"How will I chop wood?" Magnus asked.

"With an axe," Glenn said, with a chuckle. "How else? There are a few in the shed behind the house."

Glenn showed Magnus the shed and let him pick one of the three axes hanging on the walls.

"I don't know how to chop wood," Magnus protested.

He chose the biggest axe, thinking it would be the fastest way to work, but the axe was heavy and awkward in his hands. He returned it and took the smallest one. Then Glenn pointed out a chopping block where Magnus could split the branches and logs that he found.

"When you don't know how to do something, just start," Glenn said. "Truly, you'll learn by doing."

Magnus thought this was lousy advice, as he struggled with his task. After an hour of chopping branches, the pile of wood at his side had hardly grown, and his arms and back ached. He paused to go in and get his leather book. He read through some of the poems and notes he had made during the journey here, but found no clues on how to chop wood. He tucked the book into his jacket, thinking he was foolish to have hoped for an answer there.

He chopped a few more branches. As he paused to wipe the sweat from his brow, a raven flew by and landed on a log beside him, cawing loudly. Again, he thought he heard the low voice whisper: *Fool.* When he looked around for the source of the voice, Magnus was startled to see that Amelia sat on a stump behind him. Some of her ragged layers of clothes fluttered slightly, as though she had just sat down and was still settling into place.

"Give me the axe," she ordered.

She stood, and Magnus handed the axe to her. With her thin arms, she effortlessly chopped several pieces of wood. She chopped more wood in a few minutes than he had in an hour.

"How old are you really?" Magnus asked. He blushed, embarrassed at how easily this elderly woman could chop wood in comparison to his paltry effort.

"I told you. A hundred and thirty years." Her deeply wrinkled face remained expressionless, but her eyes were piercing. She dropped the axe and turned and walked away. For two or three seconds, she seemed to rise above the earth with both her feet.

"Hey!" he shouted. He leapt forward and caught up to her. "Did you just levitate?"

"I spend too much time with birds," she responded.

She continued walking, each foot clearly touching the earth. Magnus wondered if it had been an optical illusion. Or, perhaps, she had found a book in The Secret Bookstore that had taught her how to fly.

"How did you do that? Is flying your purpose?" he called after her.

She glanced back at him.

"My purpose has not yet been revealed to me. When you've lived as long as I have, you don't worry about such things anymore," she said, impatiently, as though she had spoken to many people like Magnus and was tired of the same questions.

"Could you teach me how to walk on water?"

"It will be easy if you stop being afraid of sinking," she said, in a tone that said this was obvious. "I don't mean be brave and confront the fear. That's courage. I mean have no fear. That's pure love."

Amelia walked on and disappeared into the darkness of the forest, as Magnus thought that it was not nearly as simple as she made it sound. But he was afraid to argue with her, and be sharply scolded again, so he said nothing.

Dragon Slaying

Moments after Amelia disappeared, Magnus decided to follow her.

He tiptoed along behind her. He hoped she was the owner of The Secret Bookstore, but sensed she would not want to be followed and he didn't want to risk her wrath again. Occasionally, he stepped on a twig or branch. Each time he did so, he froze. But she never looked behind her for the source of the sound. He thought that perhaps at her age, her hearing wasn't sharp. Or, perhaps, because the forest was full of creaking branches and bird-song, his steps were not noticeable.

Where possible he walked in the shadows of trees and hid behind trunks or undergrowth, so if she looked back, she would not see him. The forest here was not very dense, and many times he knew he would be clearly visible in spots of sunlight.

About five minutes later, Amelia stopped at and entered a Gothic-like mansion of decaying black wood. Magnus didn't want to knock on her front door and reveal his presence; instead he sat on a log behind the cover of a screen of tall ferns to study the mansion. He planned to return later that day or in the days ahead, when he knew she was not there, to slip inside to look for the bookstore.

As he considered returning to Glenn's house, Magnus looked down at the log he was sitting on. It had what looked like hieroglyphics carved into it. Magnus imagined that the soft, flowing letters or symbols might have been written by elves. After studying them for a few minutes, he realized that they were identical to the tattoos on Glenn's arms and the mysterious language in Glenn's book.

He took out his journal from his jacket pocket, and copied some of the tree hieroglyphs into it, hoping they might contain a clue to the location of the bookstore. While writing, he sensed someone's nearby presence. He looked up to see Amelia seated on a log a few feet away, watching him.

"Come," Amelia said. She gestured with a brusque movement of her hand.

He wondered how long she'd been there, as he stood and loosened his stiff knee. He moved like an old man, as she sprinted ahead to the open clearing in front of her house.

Two turkey vultures sat in an open upstairs window of Amelia's home. A third sat on her rooftop. She took Magnus into her house and told him to look around. Downstairs she lived in only three rooms: a bedroom, a kitchen and a living room. All the other rooms were completely empty, with only some spider webs in the corners, and wooden floors covered with dust and dried leaves. None of the rooms held any books.

Likewise, upstairs she showed him room after empty room. In several the windows were broken and chickadees flew in and out, as though they owned the place. Their bold flight both proved and created their faith that no barriers existed. Magnus wished he could be that brave. Instead, when he reached out, expecting hard glass or a wall, he touched what he sought.

Finally, she showed him the last empty room. Magnus was disappointed that this one too had no books; instead a vulture sat in the windowsill. It stood, spread out its wings and flew away as they entered.

As Magnus walked through the room, one of his feet sank through a rotting floor board. He froze. The raven swooshed past him, landing on the windowsill, where the vulture had sat moments before. Its black feathers were iridescent in a ray of sunlight. Amelia stood in the doorway with her hands on her hips, layers of skirts fluttering around her.

"You really aren't hiding the bookstore here," Magnus said.

"No." She smoothed down one of her ragged layers of skirts.

"Amelia, this house is disintegrating around you. It could collapse at any time." Magnus wiggled his foot out of the floor and tiptoed back to the hallway. "It's not safe."

"What? I should worry about death? Isn't death part of life

at my age?" She cackled. Then she gestured brusquely again. "Come."

Amelia took Magnus to a river directly behind her house. Several feet from the water's edge she showed him an enormous tree, seemingly identical to the ancient trees Magnus had seen when he had first entered the forest. She gestured to the ground beneath the branches and they sat side by side, leaning against the huge trunk. As she shifted several of the layers of her skirts, he caught a peek of her thin stick-like ankles above her boots; she was as delicately boned as a bird.

Magnus could not see the beauty in the steadily moving clear water. As he realized that large bodies of water still made him feel somewhat uneasy, he sighed in disappointment with himself that he wasn't any braver yet.

"You're heavy on your feet like a clumsy newborn calf," she noted. "I could hear you crashing behind me through the forest. Hasn't Glenn taught you anything?"

"The boy is better at learning how to track," Magnus said. "But tell me, honestly, do you know where the bookstore is?"

"Come," Amelia said. "Let me show you something else."

She stood. Reluctantly, he stood too and followed her to the edge of the river. She pointed to the heavy darkness of the forest on the other side of the water. He ignored the fear building in his chest as he stood beside her.

"I never go over there. That's where the dragon lives," she said.

"Does it breathe fire?" he asked, raising his eyebrows.

"Look for the smoke."

Because she spoke seriously, Magnus looked more closely this time, thinking perhaps she saw some mist rising up from the land. He still saw nothing, except trees and darkness.

"Dragons don't exist," he said firmly, and crossed his arms in front of him.

"What's a good story without a dragon?" Amelia asked. "And an even better story is when the hero slays the dragon. There's no bridge anywhere on the river. You'll have to walk across the water to get over there. That would be the best story of all."

She looked meaningfully at Magnus, and he felt her silently asking him to be courageous. He shuffled backwards.

"Yes, you're in a story," Amelia said. She poked his chest with a bony finger, looking just like a witch, so Magnus was glad that she was good. "You don't want to be the hero, and you don't want to slay a dragon. Well, maybe you'll be lucky and just outwit the dragon, instead of fighting it. That's boring for all of us who are watching, including the reader, but easier for you."

"I'm not a hero," Magnus said, unfolding his arms. "Truly, I'm a coward."

"Then who is going to take care of that dragon?" Amelia asked. "Glenn? An old man? Or the boy? Me? An old lady who's barely four foot tall?"

Magnus felt even more cowardly, as he looked down as his feet and inched backwards. He thought he might mention his knee injury as an excuse. He immediately knew that this tough, old bird-woman would not accept excuses as weak as that.

"I don't believe in dragons," he said, slowly. He was unsure if he was trying to convince her or himself.

"But you believe in secret bookstores?"

Magnus opened and closed his mouth several times. Finally, he said: "Glenn never mentioned a dragon."

"Of course not. Would you have come with him, if he had? Consider this though—don't we all have dragons in our own hearts?"

"So it's not a real dragon?" Magnus asked, and sighed in relief.

"Anything we have to overcome is real enough. Come. I'll show you something else."

After a few steps, she stopped and pointed the opposite way into the forest behind her decaying house.

"What am I looking for?" Magnus asked.

"More dragons."

"How many are there?"

"Look. There's more smoke. More challenges. Things you still have to overcome. Defeat them, and you'll find the bookstore."

"So the store isn't over the river?" Magnus frowned, thinking Amelia spoke in riddles, much like Glenn.

"It's wherever your dragon is."

"I don't know about the dragon, but I have been hearing a voice." He hesitated. "A deep male voice. And sometimes I see a shadowy figure slipping away. Glenn never sees the shadow or hears the voice. Is there a real person following me?"

Amelia stared into the dark undergrowth of the forest without answering.

"Well? Am I imagining things?" Magnus asked.

"It's not my job to tell you who or what is real. All I know with certainty is that we see exactly what we are looking for. Who's to say what you're seeing and hearing isn't a dragon of sorts? Come."

Magnus expected her to bring him into her home again. Instead she brought him to a shed behind her house, where she kept carrier pigeons.

"Next time you hide around my home, stalking me, I'll set you to work cleaning out the cages," she said. "Anytime you're hungry, I'll feed you. But in exchange you clean out the cages."

Magnus looked skeptical, and edged backwards.

"You're thinking there are few worse jobs." She jabbed at his chest again. "I see you trying to slip away. I'm old, but I'm not blind. I've cleaned out these cages many times over the years. There's no shame in hard, honest work. In the moment that you're doing something, whatever it is, that's your purpose."

"How old are you really?"

"At least a hundred and thirty years old," she said. "Give or take a few decades. Certainly old enough to know that a world with dragons is far more interesting than a world without them."

The Elderly Couple

The next morning, as Glenn prepared to leave with Elliott to again look for the intruder cutting down trees, an elderly couple strolled up to the house. The man had the woman's gold purse slung over his shoulder. She wore a floppy hat with a cloth daisy sewn on the front. Magnus went out to meet them. The man showed Magnus a business card. In surprise Magnus read: *The Secret Bookstore.* Before Magnus could explain that he too was looking for the store, Glenn appeared at his side.

"I'm just leaving," Glenn told the couple. "Magnus will give you a book from my shelves—something to enjoy while you're looking for the store."

Glenn took Elliott's hand and walked away. Magnus ran after them.

"Wait. Which one should I give them?" Magnus whispered to Glenn. "You should choose one for them."

"Look into their hearts and pick the one they need based on that," Glenn said.

"What does that mean?" Magnus plucked at Glenn's sleeve as Glenn continued walking.

"Like a doctor?" Elliott asked, looking puzzled. "He has to do heart surgery?"

"In a way," Glenn said, and chuckled, his eyes sparkling. "There's a throne behind the house, just under your bedroom window. Sit on it. Close your eyes and visualize the couple and then the bookshelf. Listen to the forest. Listen to the silence inside of you. And you'll just know."

"I certainly become odd in my old age," Magnus said as Glenn and Elliott walked away.

"Odd, but wise," Glenn called back.

"What about me? In my young age? Am I wise too?" Elliott asked. He grinned mischievously, and his blue eyes sparkled as brightly as Glenn's.

"You're too wise for your own good," Magnus said.

"Robin agrees with you," Elliott called back.

Magnus invited the couple into the house and seated them at the kitchen table. The table was made of wide boards that Glenn had hammered together. It had once been sanded and varnished, but it had seen many years of use and was now crisscrossed with scratches and stains. The man admired the craftsmanship of the table. The woman admired how it had been worn.

"Gives it character," she said. "Everything old should have character. People included."

The man nodded in agreement, placing the gold purse before him on the table.

As Magnus prepared them coffee, he wondered if perhaps they wanted a book on immortality or eternal youth. Glenn had not forbidden him from asking questions, so Magnus asked directly, "What kind of book are you looking for?"

"Now that we're old, we'd like to know what the purpose of the rest of our lives is," the woman said.

Her pale skin wasn't so much wrinkled, as creased with age. She reminded Magnus of his deceased maternal grandmother. She had read stories to him for hours. She had been his favourite person in the world. As a child he had assumed the only purpose she had in the world was to read to him. Now looking at this woman before him, he realized that although she had died twenty-five years ago, he still missed his grandmother.

"There are a lot of things we could do," the man said, leaning forward and resting his hands on the table, beside the woman's purse. "But which ones should we do? Why are we still alive?"

"I told Norman—my husband—that when people live into old age it isn't to wait around waiting for death. They still have a definite purpose," the woman said. "If we're still alive, then there must be a reason."

"Trudy has never been wrong," Norman added, looking tenderly at his wife. "I once saw a five-hundred-year old tree at the edge of a field. It was never cut down because it was alive, healthy and old, and therefore respected. But even that tree had to produce new leaves each spring to show it was still living."

"And how can you know that you're living, unless there's movement of life around you?" Trudy asked. "Dear young man, there is no full life lived in isolation."

Magnus liked the couple, and he very much wanted to help them. Once the coffee was ready, he gave them each a mug and excused himself to find the throne that Glenn had told him to sit on. Under his bedroom window, he found a stump of a maple tree. Part of the stump had broken away, leaving a natural back, so it looked like a mini-throne. Green moss covered most of the stump, but the seat was smooth and clean. On the seat there were markings identical to Glenn's tattoos and to those on the log by Amelia's house.

"A wooden throne," Magnus muttered, laughing at Glenn. Magnus laughed again, at himself this time, for expecting something more. Magnus sat on the stump. The back of it reached the bottom of his shoulder blades.

A vulture flew over the clearing around Glenn's house, and Magnus nodded at it, acknowledging the bird's presence. The bird flew so low he could hear the soft swoosh of each wing flapping.

Magnus closed his eyes. First, he visualized the bird flying. Then he heard the sounds of the forest: the distant caw of a crow, a chattering squirrel, rustling leaves, the hum of a mosquito. These sounds disappeared inside of him as he listened to the sound of the bird's silent flight above. He had thought there was no sound within silence. Instead, he found that silence roared with so much noise, it was an unearthly sound. Silence had a presence as thick as water. It was easy to move through, but hard to resist its flow. For Magnus this silence was a new language, as unique and hard to decipher as the hieroglyphics of Glenn's tattoos.

The stump felt warm against his back and he felt himself sort of settling into the wood, the stump holding him up.

Magnus visualized the bookshelves in Glenn's living room. He saw a tiny pinpoint of light dancing across the book in which he had written a poem last night. He could imagine no other book for the elderly couple.

Smiling slightly, he returned to the house and stood in front of the bookshelves. For a moment he thought he saw a mouse scurrying over the same book. When he looked directly at it, the imagined mouse disappeared. However, the pinpoint of light shone on the book again. He pulled out the book and in a way he could not explain, it felt like the right weight and texture and size and colour as he held it in his hand.

He did have the ability to choose a book. Glenn had been correct. Perhaps Glenn wasn't as odd as he thought. Or perhaps he, himself, was becoming as odd as Glenn. He didn't mind either way.

He brought the book to the waiting couple. Trudy eagerly

took the book and glanced through it. She read the poem at the back.

Burial of the Earth

the worn-out sun
                                        bleeds

away
            falls
                        the day

the sky
cracks

night spreads
thinly

disguised
as the ancient mother's
robes

the old
child
brings
              offerings
his sacrifice
       of grasstwigsstringmud

rescued
bird nests

"I wrote that," Magnus said, apologetically. "There's the boy, Elliott, who collects bits of this and that and—."

"Young man, it's perfect," Trudy said. "This is it. We need look no farther."

"No, no!" Magnus protested. He reached out to take the book back. "This isn't the bookstore you're looking for. You can find the right book if you keep searching. Maybe I could help you. I'm also looking for the store."

Trudy stepped away from Magnus and passed the book to her husband, Norman. He put on reading glasses and also read the poem. Then he nodded slowly.

"We need look no farther," he said, echoing Trudy. "We're done searching."

Trudy gave Magnus a tight hug, and thanked him. Then she and Norman left holding hands. The man again slung the woman's purse over his shoulder. Magnus was perplexed. He wondered what was in the book that made them so content.

When Glenn and Elliott returned that evening, Magnus told them what had happened.

"What's the problem?" Glenn asked. He set the sack full of walnuts and beech nuts that they had gathered that day on the kitchen table. "They got a book they're happy with."

"What if I led them astray on their search?" Magnus asked, his voice rising.

Elliott ran in and grabbed a handful of nuts and tossed them in his pail. The point of his party hat had been pushed down and it now looked like a lopsided volcano. His bare feet slapped loudly against the wooden floors, as he ran out the kitchen, went down the hall and into his bedroom.

"Maybe they were meant to meet someone else," Magnus said, and his shoulders slumped. "I think I accidentally misled them."

"Twenty years ago I left the forest for a week and wandered about the city," Glenn said. "I was blessed to meet some wonderful people. But then I left them and returned home to the forest."

"What does that mean?" Magnus asked.

"That week the detour was my only destination."

"By definition a detour can't be a destination."

"You're right," Glenn said, agreeing with Magnus for the first time that he could remember.

Magnus straightened his back.

"Finally," Magnus said.

"But only partially right," Glenn continued. "While that might usually be true, if people are really awake and alive like that couple, the unexpected detour always makes the destination unnecessary. If, after they accepted the detour, they pursued the destination, the destination would become the detour."

Magnus paused to try to understand Glenn, but Glenn interrupted his thoughts: "That's enough debating. You're not ready yet to outwit me completely. Let's make supper. You have the fire going in the stove? Good. Elliott has two rabbits outside that I snared and they need to be cleaned and roasted."

Book Graveyard

The next day Glenn wanted Magnus to help him look for the person cutting down the trees, and left Elliott behind to gather acorns with Amelia. He insisted that Amelia was more than trustworthy enough to take care of the boy.

After an hour walking through the forest, Glenn and Magnus came to a large clearing where the ground was lower than normal and the air smelled putrid. White stones of various shapes and sizes dotted the area.

In the middle of the clearing, a man was digging a hole with a shovel, as he sobbed. Beside him lay something wrapped in a blue blanket. Magnus guessed a beloved dog or cat had died. Three children stood trembling in a row just behind the man. Their faces were solemn, as they clutched each other's hands.

"No looking back, no looking back, no looking back," the man muttered. Long strands of uncombed black hair fell across his cheeks, hiding his face.

Magnus and Glenn silently and slowly approached the man.

When the weeping man noticed them, he stopped digging. The oldest child, a boy of about eleven, lifted a corner of the blanket to reveal a book. Magnus was surprised when he saw the object. He leaned closer to read the title: *Alice in Wonderland.*

Quickly, the man covered the book up again, gently put it in the hole and shovelled dirt over it. When he'd filled the hole, the middle child, a girl of about eight, handed the man a white rock, which he reverently laid at the head of the place where he had just buried the book. The youngest, a girl of about four, patted the rock with a plump hand and then stood beside her father. The still-weeping man stood. He took a strand of his lank hair and used it to wipe his cheeks.

"See that large rock?" he said to Magnus and Glenn. He pointed to a corner of the clearing. "There lies *War and Peace.* The bigger the stone, the longer the book."

The man mentioned several Russian politicians who had written autobiographies, whose books he had also buried there. Magnus didn't recognize the names, but nodded, pretending to know who the man was talking about.

"Magnus is not up-to-date on Russian history," Glenn said, laughing at his own joke.

"Ha, ha." Magnus faked a laugh. Then he shook his head and smiled. Glenn's sense of humour was growing on him.

To turn the topic away from Russian history and out of curiosity, Magnus pointed at the largest rock in the middle of the clearing. "And that one?"

"The one story I wrote myself. My autobiography. It's just five pages long, but one's own story is always the most important, isn't it?"

Magnus' heart leapt, as he thought he finally had found The Secret Bookstore. He congratulated himself for having the courage to make this journey. He straightened his shoulders and it seemed his knee stopped aching instantly. Energy surged through his torso and limbs.

"Is this your bookstore?" Magnus eagerly asked the man.

"Are you mad? This is a graveyard of books," the man said, gruffly, spearing the earth near his feet with the point of his shovel.

Magnus thought that if anyone was mad it was this man, who was burying books as if they were dead bodies. But he kept his silence. He glanced at the children, who still stood in a solemn row, holding hands again.

Beside him, Glenn squatted down and with a bony finger brushed aside a dried oak leaf, and then touched what looked like a clod of dirt. The dirt seemed to move. Magnus looked more closely and saw that it was a brown toad that had puffed out its sides.

"These are books you didn't like?" Magnus asked, ignoring Glenn and the toad.

"To the contrary. Many, many years ago, I spent five years reading and rereading one book," the man said. "Then someone gave me a new book. But I couldn't stop reading the old one. I was addicted to the story. So my wife took it, wrapped it in a piece of old cloth and buried it. She said I couldn't read the old book again until I had read the new one. But I was compelled to read the new one over and over again too. Finally, at my wife's insistence, I agreed to bury every book after I read it."

"Why don't you give them away?" Magnus asked, still hoping this might be The Secret Bookstore. "Give them to people who really want them."

"I couldn't ask people to suffer like I have, addicted to re-reading one book over and over, as though that were the only one in the world. People should make room for new stories." The man wiped tears from his face again using his long hair.

Continuing to stare at the toad, Glenn stood and whispered to Magnus: "A common mistake—he thinks everyone behaves and thinks just like himself."

"This really isn't The Secret Bookstore?" Magnus whispered back.

"Most of the books here are rotted to nothing," Glenn said. He smoothed his beard with his hand. "This is no store."

Magnus caught himself imitating Glenn, smoothing his own short beard which had grown out since they left the city.

"You could throw them out or burn them," Magnus said aloud. He cringed as soon as he said this, hating the idea of a book burning, wishing he could take the words back again.

"But here they might be raised up again into something

better," the man said. "People have souls. So do animals and trees. Why not books? Once they're buried, maybe they can rise up as perfect new stories for anyone in the world to enjoy."

The man picked up a black top hat that lay on the ground near the children, and put it on. He lifted the youngest child onto his shoulders. Then he took the hands of the other two children, and walked away from the book graveyard.

"No looking back," the man chanted. "No looking back. No looking back."

"It's all right, Daddy. We've got lots more books at home," the girl on his shoulders said.

"Yes," he shouted. "We can start reading a new book today. We'll have popcorn to celebrate. It's party time!"

The children cheered as they and their father ran down the path.

Toad

In a trance, Magnus stared at the fresh book grave. He imagined himself digging up books to find one about walking on water. Glenn startled him out of his reverie by nudging his arm.

Magnus stepped back, and the toad leapt at his sudden movement. Startled by the creature, Magnus stumbled backwards and fell. He hadn't expected that fat body with its stubby legs to overcome inertia so easily.

The toad had jumped onto the fresh grave, and its squat face imitated Glenn's, its mouth in the same straight serious line. Its bumpy brown skin made it almost invisible against the brown soil.

As he stood up, Magnus imagined that Elliott would have loved the toad, and would have added it to his pail as a treasure.

"There'll be no book here about how to walk on water," Glenn said quietly.

"Why do you think I destroyed all the poems I've written,

until I met you?" Magnus asked, fidgeting with his walking stick. He sniffed the air. While the sun had dissipated the morning mist, the air still smelled like decay. Staring at the toad, Magnus thought of all his shredded poems. None of them had been buried. None of them was marked with a stone. None was even marked with as much as a pebble or twig.

"I don't know."

"Because I'm not a poet," Magnus answered his own question.

"That certainly makes sense," Glenn said. "Only poets should write and keep their poems. Everyone else who writes poetry should destroy their poems. Or bury them as deeply as possible."

Magnus glanced at him to see if he was being sarcastic, but Glenn's face was impassive, like the toad's. Magnus wondered, as he had many times before, what Glenn thought of him, and if Glenn actually liked him. Was Glenn glad that he had become a tattooed man with a long beard who lived in a forest, instead of a wealthy accountant? As though hearing his thoughts, Glenn's lips turned up in a slight smile, and he pushed up the sleeves of his fall jacket and with a finger traced some of the tattoos on his right arm.

"Even so, I should have written a poem in exchange for this walking stick right away, instead of trying to clean out the horse stall," Magnus said, lifting the stick in the air. "It would have been much easier."

Glenn didn't answer. His silence surprised Magnus. He had expected Glenn to tell him that he should never take the easy road. He dropped the stick to his side. He liked the feel of it his hand; having it nearby made him feel strong.

Glenn continued tracing his tattoos with his index finger.

"There are many things I don't understand," Glenn said at last. "Many answers that I don't have. Many questions I don't know how to ask."

"Do you think books have souls?" Magnus asked.

"Books only live when people are reading them," Glenn answered, rolling down his sleeves. "As long as their pages can still be read, I assume they would still have life in them."

Glenn walked away.

Magnus bent and stroked the toad's bumpy back with one finger, as he thought of all the poems he had written that no one had ever read and he had never wanted anyone to read. His right eyelid twitched.

"I don't know why I'm uneasy," Magnus whispered to the toad.

The toad flicked out its tongue and ate a tiny fly in response. Magnus admired his quick decisive movement.

"You're full of hidden talents," Magnus said softly. "But do you exist because there are flies to eat? Or do flies exist to provide you with food? Vultures only eat what has already died. I wonder if they're proud of not being predators?"

"What was that?" Glenn called back.

"Just talking to this handsome toad." Magnus stood, rubbing his brow. "He's quite charming. Elliott would love him."

"What did it say?"

Suddenly wanting to leave the putrid book graveyard, Magnus ran to catch up to Glenn.

"Nothing. I wish he had said something. I wish just one animal would tell me something. Those damn turkey vultures never say a thing," Magnus said, pointing at several sitting in a tree. The birds stood and shifted. "They're so quiet."

"Their appearance is the only words you'll get from them. That should be enough. Consider that this spring I walked through a field of dandelions, all gone to seed, fuzzy white heads nodding wisely as old men. I sensed they were nodding in approval. I was very peaceful that day."

"That must mean something," Magnus said. "But I don't know what. When do I start talking in such riddles? And when will I understand them?"

"If you write a poem about it, you'll figure it out," Glenn said.

"Yes," Magnus agreed. "Unexpected answers come to me when I'm writing."

Falling Leaves

The next day started out in darkness.

And as the sky remained overcast, to Magnus it felt like the sun never rose.

Later that afternoon at a pond near Glenn's house, Glenn and Magnus sat and watched maple leaves fall into the water. The pond was a small enough body of water that Magnus felt no anxiety about it. He pushed aside some leaves on the ground with his walking stick. A tiny snake slithered from under the leaves and into the pond. Magnus noted to himself that he didn't jump at the snake's movement and the reptile didn't repulse him.

"Yes," Glenn said. "You're getting used to wildlife and living outdoors. Soon you won't even need me at all."

"At first it was disturbing when you read my thoughts," Magnus said, continuing to watch the snake gliding through the water. "But now I like it. It almost feels comforting. It's like I'm never alone."

"You never are alone. But that's not because I'm here."

"What do you mean?"

"Listen, I have something else to tell you. Something to show you. Look there." With his walking stick Glenn gestured at the leaves clinging to the tree. The morning sun shone through them, so some of the veins were visible. "Truly, they're all going to fall. And not one is hurt when it lands. Some just let go. Others are ripped away by the wind. Others resist leaving the tree long into the winter. But even those last ones will descend.

"I have never seen a leaf broken by its fall. And if it was broken, it would not shatter."

Magnus pondered Glenn's words as he stared at a yellow leaf shivering at the end of a branch. It was low enough to touch, so he reached out and pulled it off. He tossed it away, and watched it drift downward into the pond. Glenn sounded more serious than he ever had been before.

"What are you really saying?" Magnus finally asked.

"The leaf will fall, whether it resists or not," Glenn said. He paused to rub a hand over his cheek. "Why not let go of the tree? It would be the easiest way."

"Perhaps the tree is holding onto the leaf," Magnus said. "And not the leaf onto the tree."

He caught himself mirroring Glenn, rubbing a hand over his own cheek, feeling his growing beard. He glanced at Glenn and then back at leaves swirling through the pond. The snake had disappeared.

"Then the tree is foolish. New leaves will come in the spring. Why hold onto the brittle and decaying?" Glenn said, his voice wavering. He loudly cleared his throat.

Magnus glanced quickly back at Glenn. He suddenly noticed that Glenn looked tired; his eyelids drooped and there were dark circles under his eyes.

"The stubborn leaves are the most beautiful for clinging there," Magnus said. He paused. He sounded like Glenn. But the words and ideas had come from inside of him. Even though he was sure that he wasn't hearing Glenn's thoughts, it seemed like the idea had come from the old man. "Their determination is their beauty."

"You're right," Glenn said, agreeing with Magnus so passionately that Magnus was surprised. "The stubborn ones are beautiful."

Something rustled in a nearby bush. Magnus turned slowly, expecting to see the shadowy figure. Instead two, then three, then five chickadees flitted from the bush to the underbrush. Glenn took several sunflower seeds out of one of his jacket pockets. He remained seated, resting his hands on his knees. Half an hour later one of the chickadees landed on Glenn's palm and took a seed. Then another bird followed and then other. Within minutes, the chickadees had eaten all the seeds.

"You made that look easy," Magnus said.

"It's just patience masquerading as talent."

Glenn tugged the end of his beard, as he stood up. Magnus couldn't be sure if he was imagining it, but it seemed Glenn's movements were slower than normal and slightly stiff. He looked older than he had yesterday. An uneasy knot formed in Magnus' stomach.

Going To A Beautiful Place

That evening at supper, Glenn cleared his throat. He said to Elliott, "I have to go soon, and I won't be back."

"Where are you going?" Elliott took a bite of the stew that Glenn had prepared.

"A place where you can only follow me when you're a very, very old man."

Elliott laughed because he couldn't imagine himself as old as Glenn. Magnus did not laugh, because he understood that Glenn meant he was dying. He could hardly manage to swallow the food he had in his mouth. His throat ached and his stomach clenched. He set his fork down beside his plate, his shoulders tightening. He leaned back from the kitchen table and moved his feet, ready to stand up and leave the room.

Then he caught Elliott observing him. To show the boy that nothing was wrong, Magnus pretended to continue eating, although he only moved food around his plate. Glenn kept his face and eyes down, but Magnus noticed that his forehead was beaded with sweat.

Abruptly, Elliott left the table to find a goodbye present for Glenn. He returned with a glass jar with three daddy-longlegs that he said he had trained to do circus tricks. Glenn thanked him as if he had just received a treasure box of gold. Elliott beamed with pride.

As he studied the creatures scurrying around in the jar, Magnus vaguely remembered himself as a young boy keeping jars holding centipedes and spiders under his bed, hiding them from his mother.

Elliott whispered to the empty chair beside him, speaking to his invisible friend.

"Robin says you're going to a beautiful place," Elliott said aloud.

"I am," Glenn agreed.

After supper, Glenn and Magnus sat outside on wooden rocking chairs near the front door. Glenn had made the simple chairs, and though they were not stained or varnished they were comfortable and solid. They looked across the clearing into the darkening forest. The sun had slipped away beneath the treeline, and the first bats were dipping and diving around them.

"I need you to find the person cutting down the trees," Glenn said after a time.

"How?" Magnus asked. He had to force the single word out of his tight throat. He was afraid he might start crying if he said more.

"Promise me that when you catch him, you'll bring him to Amelia. She'll help you take care of the tree-cutter. She may be old, but she'll be able to deal with him. That's all you need do when you find this person. Don't take care of things yourself. Promise me."

Glenn's voice was softer than normal, and he sounded weary. Magnus didn't dare turn his gaze from the forest to look at Glenn's face. He could sense Glenn was fading, but he didn't want to see it.

"How will I find the person cutting down the trees, or the bookstore or Matilda without you?" Magnus asked in a rush. His heart thumped in his chest and his hands grew clammy. He rubbed them on his pants.

"Elliott can teach you how to track the person and the bookstore. He knows more than enough to help you find both."

"He's just a child," Magnus protested.

"He's been paying attention and learning quickly."

"I need you to stay." Magnus' voice broke. He cleared his throat. "Not just to find the bookstore—. I'll miss you."

"These bones are old and ready for a new purpose."

"You're wrong," Magnus said.

It felt like his heart was ripping into pieces.

Life And Death Dance

The next morning Glenn said, "Elliott, I need you to teach Magnus everything you know about tracking."

Glenn was sitting up in his bed, his head resting against several plump pillows.

"Sure," Elliott said, and ran from the room to the front door.

"You'll still be here when we get back?" Magnus asked. He stared hard at Glenn, as though he could look through his eyes into his soul.

"I'll be here," Glenn said. His eyes met Magnus', but Glenn's eyes were not intense like they once had been. They were soft, watery. His skin was paler than normal. "I'm fine right now, just tired."

Magnus looked around Glenn's bedroom, as though it might hold some answer to what he should do—stay here with Glenn or go tracking with the child. A large window opposite his bed let in natural light. All the walls were bare, without pictures or photographs. In one corner stood a wooden chair. He had a small armoire of chestnut wood opposite his bed. Set into one wall was a small fireplace. On three hooks on the wall beside the door hung a bearskin coat, a light fall jacket and a pair of deerskin pants. Beside Glenn's bed, his walking stick rested against the wall.

Magnus knew he would have to make his own decisions from now on, and agreed to go out tracking with Elliott. Elliott took along his pail and a thin red string to hold up to detect the direction of the wind. He left behind his birthday hat. It had a small tear in it and the elastic that tied under his chin had broken, so it no longer stayed on his head when he ran. It was more like a flat meadow now than a mountain.

As they walked away from the house towards a ridge that edged a ravine, Elliott pointed out a lynx paw print in the earth.

"Glenn says that to find the lynx we have to pretend we are the lynx," Elliott said, crouching down. "Look at what the lynx saw. Smell what it smelled. See where it walked."

The boy moved forward on his hands and knees until he found a distant second print. Magnus walked along side of him.

"It's easy," Elliott said. He tossed a twig into the air. "It's like a game."

"I wish it was easy," Magnus muttered, shaking his head. "I came to find a bookstore, not wild animals or some trespasser cutting down trees."

He added silently to himself, *And I didn't expect to be taking care of a child.*

Aloud he said, "You're smarter than I am."

Elliott laughed and ran to point out another footprint. They followed the tracks until Elliott paused at a point where the lynx made a sharp turn to the west, away from the ravine.

"Why do you think that is?" Magnus asked. "Did it see a rabbit or squirrel? Or was it turning away from danger?"

"Glenn told me we can ask questions, but we can't expect answers," Elliott said.

"He's a wise man," Magnus said. "Where did you first meet him?"

"I don't remember." Elliott shrugged his thin shoulders. "I guess I've always known him."

"Have you always known me?"

"I've heard stories about you." Elliott giggled. "But we just met a few days ago. You can't fool me!"

"What did you hear about me?" Magnus asked, his curiosity piqued.

"Nothing." Elliott laughed again and turned away from Magnus.

"Where are your parents?"

"At home." Elliott bent to pick up the pebble he'd kicked and threw it into some underbrush. Spots of sunlight filtering through the trees danced across his face.

As Magnus thought again of Glenn dying, he felt a sharp pang of grief, remembering the death of his own father and mother. He had taken only a few days off from his job after they had passed away. Afraid of getting lost in sadness, he had instead lost himself in longer and longer hours of work. The fatigue of work had numbed him to any feelings.

Elliott picked up several more pebbles, and tossed these into his pail. "These are for my mom."

"Don't you think they miss you?"

"Nah." Fear flickered over Elliott's face. "Am I going to get in trouble? Have I been gone too long?"

"No, of course not," Magnus soothed. He pushed away his grief, wanting to be cheerful and strong for the boy.

They were in a patch of light, a gap in the canopy of trees, where the sun reached the forest floor. It caused Elliott's hair to glow like gold.

Elliott leapt forward, and pointed at a small splatter of blood and a tuft of rabbit fur. Tears flooded his cheeks. Magnus pulled him away from the scene of the lynx's meal. As he hugged the boy, the enormous shadow of a turkey vulture passed over him. A chill ran across Magnus' skin. Then he looked up, and saw the truth. Although the bird was large, six feet across from wing tip to wing tip, the angle of the morning sun had made its shadow look far larger.

"Life and death dance and embrace each other and then part as they must," Magnus said, watching the vulture fly away, letting Elliott go. "Then we put one in the grave. But let us hope we put death in the grave, and not life. Too often people get the two confused."

"Is that a poem?" Elliott said, sniffing. He wiped his nose on his sleeve.

"It will be," said Magnus, as he realized that he sounded like Glenn.

"The lynx has to eat too, right?" asked Elliott. He hiccupped.

"You'd be just as sad if the lynx starved," Magnus said, for he realized the boy was strong and wise enough to understand such things.

Elliott cocked his head, deep in thought, and then straightened. He wiped his remaining tears from his eyes with the back of his hand.

"Why does Glenn have to go away?"

"I don't know."

"I wish he'd stay," Elliott said, and then ran on through the trees.

"Me too," Magnus said softly, once the child was out of earshot. "But I think he's dancing with death and he doesn't seem to mind."

Magnus followed behind more slowly, his hands behind his back, his neck bowed. A lump of sadness caught in his throat. He tried to focus on the forest, tracking and following Elliott, but he kept thinking of Glenn in bed and remembering how old and tired he looked.

They spent the rest of the morning wandering through the

forest, looking for animal tracks and gathering rocks, moss, and insects to add to Elliott's pail. Magnus refrained from asking Elliott any more questions about his past. But if Glenn died now, Magnus worried about what he'd do with the boy.

Searching For A Doctor

The next morning Glenn coughed frequently, and said that he was too tired to get out of bed. He told Magnus that he felt as though someone had hit him just below his shoulder blades, and he could feel a slight gurgling in his chest and lower back.

Magnus felt Glenn's brow. His skin was hot to the touch, like he had a fever.

Magnus wanted to take him to a hospital, but Glenn insisted that he was too tired to go anywhere.

"If you tell me the way out of the forest, I'll bring a doctor here," Magnus promised.

In response Glenn closed his eyes. Magnus stood and waited beside his bed. Glenn was lying flat, his green woolen blanket tucked up to his chin. His beard was outside the blanket and rose and fell on his chest with his breathing. Magnus touched Glenn's carved walking stick, which was still leaning against the wall beside the bed.

The silence between them unravelled. Magnus shifted his

feet and put more weight on his strong left leg. As the silence stretched out even longer, Magnus felt something inside begin to fray. He realized Glenn wasn't going to tell him how to leave the forest, and he visualized the silence as a red ball of yarn tangled around them.

"I see your eyelids fluttering. I know you're awake," Magnus said.

Glenn kept his eyes closed and didn't speak. Magnus leaned so close to Glenn that he could hear his breathing.

"You're being childish," Magnus said.

The corners of Glenn's lips twitched.

"I'm just a flickering candle now," Glenn said.

"I'll find a way without you." As Magnus left the bedroom, he thought he heard Glenn speak behind him. But when he paused in the hall outside the door to listen, all he heard again was the unravelling red ball of silence.

Magnus found Amelia kneeling in her vegetable garden in front of her home. She was digging up carrots. Her raven stood amongst the row of soft green tops. As Magnus neared, the bird flew up towards him. Magnus jumped to the side, and batted it away with his hands.

"Crazy bird," he said, impatiently.

The raven cawed and flew to sit in an open window of the

house. A rotted piece of wood fell from the window sill to the ground.

"I need help," Magnus called to Amelia. "Glenn is sick. How do I get out of the forest? I need a doctor."

"Already?" she asked.

He jogged the remaining steps to her.

"What do you mean 'already'?" Magnus demanded.

He reached her side, and stood close beside her. Her sharp eyes moistened with tears. She bent her head, and, still kneeling, leaned onto the shovel at her side. She ignored Magnus' offered hand, and pulled herself up. Clumps of dry dirt clung to the layers of ragged skirts at her knees.

"I'll come to see him, but I can't guide you out," she said. She cleared her throat and pulled a wisp of hair away from her eyes.

"You don't know the way?" Magnus asked, surprised.

"There are many paths out of the forest. I know them all. But Glenn doesn't want to go back to the city. He's happy here," she said in a soft voice.

"He could die!" His voice rose. His words caught in his throat and a lump grew there. "Do you understand? We have to do something. Truly, you must be able to do something to help? Maybe some herbal remedy?"

An image of his parents in the coffins at their funeral flashed through his mind. There had been a snowstorm. His mother had been driving because his father's eyesight had deteriorated and he couldn't see well at night. The police officer told Magnus that she probably had hit black ice. No other cars were involved. They crashed into a tree. Someone discovered the car the next morning. The coroner said that they both died instantly on impact; however, for months afterwards Magnus had nightmares that they had survived the accident and had bled or frozen to death, while waiting and hoping for help to arrive.

"I can't help him," Amelia said, firmly, turning her head to look towards the river.

"I'll give you anything," Magnus pleaded, clenching his hands into fists. "Everything I own, if you'll show me how to get to a hospital. I can't just let Glenn die. He's not just some old man I met. He's my friend. He's like a father to me. He is me."

"I already have everything I need," Amelia said. "And Glenn has everything he needs."

"He needs a doctor," Magnus' voice rose.

"He's not afraid." Amelia cleared her throat again. She continued to look toward the river, avoiding his eyes. "It's not unusual for old people to feel in their soul when the time has arrived. They put things in order and lie in bed and just go. He'd rather you let him leave peacefully."

Magnus swallowed hard several times so he wouldn't shout. But his voice did squeak with anger when he said, "You told me to be brave enough to fight dragons. How can you expect me to just sit with him and watch him die like a coward?"

The raven flew from the house and landed on top of the pile of dug-up carrots. It made a guttural sound, as if clearing its voice, and hopped from foot to foot. Amelia ignored the bird, continuing to stare at the river.

"Whose fault will it be if he dies?" Magnus demanded.

"I'm not a coward," Amelia said. "If he's ready to go, it's my job to see him off. That takes some courage."

She turned from Magnus, but not before he saw a tear slip down her weathered cheek. As it disappeared into the wrinkled loose skin at her neck, the raven flew to her shoulder. Magnus moved to stand in front of her.

Her eyes were again like glass flowers. Only now they were cracked.

He continued to plead, argue and cajole. She continued to refuse to help him. Finally, he stormed away from her.

"I'll find the way out myself!" he shouted at her as he left the clearing.

Finding His Way

Blinded by anger and fear, Magnus marched quickly and furiously through the forest. Birds scattered around him. Soon all the trees looked the same to him, but he was too upset to care that he no longer knew which way was forward and which was backward.

He grabbed two sticks and pounded a stump, until the sticks broke apart in his hands. He found two thicker sticks and pounded the trunk of an oak tree, until they too snapped into pieces. Then he grabbed two more sticks and hit tree trunks as he walked, kicking dried leaves up before him. When these sticks also broke, he dropped the remaining pieces and bent over to catch his breath. The cool air was chilly on his sweaty skin. When he stood up, he looked up through the gaps between the tree tops to see a turkey vulture flying above.

In that instant, the bird was not alone in the sky and he was not alone on the earth. Awareness of the other's presence was acknowledgement of the other's life, and this connection gave him courage. Some of his rage at Amelia and Glenn subsided. "There is no flying backwards," he said aloud to himself. "No walking backwards."

He turned his eyes from the sky to his feet. For the first time on his journey Magnus really looked at the forest floor. He had been so focused on finding The Secret Bookstore that he had never looked down and seen the forest as Glenn or Elliott had. All he had ever looked for were tree roots or rocks, so he wouldn't trip.

He noticed the layers of leaves, and how the musty scent of their decomposition rose when he nudged them with his toe. A wind blew some of the top layer of leaves so they fluttered upwards, and it looked like the floor breathed.

Dappled sunlight filtered through the trees and descended onto the forest floor, shining on a small red cardinal feather that moved. Surprised, Magnus bent down to look more closely. Two ants dragged it forward. Magnus saw the feather through Elliott's eyes—a bright, colourful treasure. The fact that ants moved it along would have thrilled the boy. For Elliott it would be something to put in his pail and keep forever—until something else beautiful caught his interest.

The forest felt smaller as Magnus studied the individual parts of it. He understood what Glenn had meant when he had referred to the skeleton of the book and the clock and said that when taken apart, each piece might be more complete than the whole. He was amazed to realize there was an entire world pulsating with life beneath his feet.

His thoughts swiftly turned back to Glenn. Although Magnus knew Glenn wanted him to accept his death, he couldn't. He couldn't let Glenn go yet. He wasn't a dying leaf. He was a person, and Magnus had to find him help.

As Magnus watched the ants with the feather, he noticed they were pulling it across deer hoof prints. He decided to follow the deer tracks, for he thought this was how Elliott might approach the journey, instead of wandering aimlessly. The child would believe there were no lost roads, just long detours.

Magnus sensed that following the tracks would bring him exactly to where he needed to be. This belief kept him walking forward with some optimism, even as the sky darkened, the sun disappearing under dark grey clouds. Even when he again thought he saw a shadowy figure darting from him through the trees, he kept moving onward, disregarding it and the sharp pain in his knee.

The tracks lead him to a log cabin with a thin thread of smoke rising from its chimney. Magnus knocked.

Matilda opened the door.

"You finally found your way!" she exclaimed, and smiled as brightly at him as she had when she saw him at the waterfront, her entire face creasing into laugh lines. "I've been waiting. I'm so glad you came."

Matilda was more petite than Magnus remembered. Her

tiny hands and feet were hardly bigger than Elliott's, and she just reached his shoulder. She wore a different dress than she had at the waterfront, but this one was also green. The same three glass-bead necklaces hung around her neck. Her curly orange hair was still unruly.

No one in his life had ever looked so happy to see him. He forgot everything else; he would not have been able to state his own name as he stared into her green eyes.

As he followed her inside the cabin, he felt light, like he could float away as easily as a balloon.

Matilda And The Beeswax Candles

The single room of the cabin smelled like honey. It was warm, in stark contrast to the cool outside air. One small window let in a little light. Half a dozen candles were lit, and a golden halo shone around each flame. Once Magnus' eyes adjusted to the dimness, he scanned the single room for books. His heart sank when, instead, he saw racks of drying herbs hanging from the ceiling, a few pieces of rough-hewn furniture, a stove with steaming pots and a table piled with long tapered candles.

"You're disappointed that I don't own The Secret Bookstore, aren't you?" Matilda asked.

Her voice was as lyrical as he remembered. As at the waterfront, she rose on her tiptoes and then sank to the balls of her feet. Then she rose up again, as if she planned to fly away.

"Yes. No. I mean—. I—.You—." Magnus fumbled with his words, blushing as he did so. He closed his eyes and spoke in a rush: "I'm happy to see you again. I believe you're real."

"The journey hasn't been easy for you."

He was relieved that she didn't laugh at him for his nervous response.

"Glenn—I need to find a doctor for Glenn," Magnus said, opening his eyes and forcing himself to concentrate, turning his mind from Matilda to the reason he had been walking through the forest. "He's—I think he's dying."

She looked concerned and nodded several times as he explained the situation and the urgency of his need to find a doctor. In his anxiety he spoke quickly, stumbling over his words, and his voice squeaked.

Instead of agreeing or arguing with him, she interrupted him by leaning forward and hugging him. He stopped speaking. Her arms were strong, and she was soft and warm against his body. The scent of honey clung to her clothes and hair.

As suddenly as she had hugged him, she released him and backed away. She tiptoed to the stove, where she stirred a pot of simmering apple cider. The sweet scent wafted towards Magnus, mixing with the smell of honey in the room. She ladled several spoonsful into a mug and handed him the cup. He took it wordlessly, struggling to find a complete thought, remembering the feeling of her body against his, even as his heart squeezed in fear about Glenn. He felt light-headed, and leaned against a log wall to keep himself upright.

"Please, sit while you let the cider cool," she said, gesturing at a wooden chair. "You need nourishment for the walk back.

While you drink, I'll clean up. I've been making beeswax candles."

"I can't. Glenn—." Magnus' voice rose again. He pressed his back harder against the wall.

She stood on tiptoes, reached up, took his face in her small soft hands and said quietly, "Trust me. Sit and drink. I have to cool the pots and smother the fire so the cabin doesn't burn down while we're gone."

She released his face and stepped backwards.

"You'll take me to a doctor?"

"Does he want a doctor?"

Magnus started to say *yes*. He stopped himself and said nothing. He couldn't lie to her.

"Hmm. I see," she said, returning to the stove.

Magnus took wobbly steps to the chair and collapsed into it.

"This pot is filled with cappings, the raw wax that came straight out of the honey comb." Matilda took a pot off the stove and set it on a thick mat on the floor. "I've been warming it slowly for days. During this time all the bits of dirt, honeycomb and dead bees have sunk to the bottom. The clean wax floats on top of the water."

As she worked, her small hands moved quickly and gracefully.

Magnus took a drink of the hot cider, and felt less lightheaded. He pressed his feet into the earthen floor and willed himself to relax. He remembered Glenn telling him that he had a hive of buzzing bees inside his head; it felt like that now. He couldn't quite think clearly or focus on one thought or feeling—his fear and sadness about Glenn, his disappointment that this wasn't The Secret Bookstore and his love and joy on finding Matilda were all jumbled together.

"I've filtered the wax this way two more times in these two other pots, to make sure it's completely clean." She removed a second and then a third pot, and set those on the mat as well. "Tonight I had planned to pour the hot wax into molds. Tomorrow, when the wax was cool and firm, I'd have removed it. But that's for another day. There. Now I'll douse the fire and we can go."

Magnus gulped down the rest of his cider, the liquid scalding his mouth. As he set the mug down on the table, something tapped lightly at the door. Matilda tiptoed to it and opened it. On the threshold sat a pigeon; Magnus knew it was a carrier pigeon because it bore a tiny tube on its leg. Matilda bent, her glass necklaces tinkling against each other as she removed the tube and from out of it took a small square of paper. She began to read it.

"It's from Amelia," she said.

Magnus jumped up.

"She writes that she's with Glenn, and that Elliott is fine."

Magnus blushed, as he realized he hadn't really thought about Elliott in his rush to help Glenn.

"How will the bird find its way back?" Magnus asked.

"I don't know, but they always do. I don't believe there's ever been a lost carrier pigeon."

Matilda sent the bird away. It flew up and disappeared into the forest. She left the door open and tiptoed back to the stove.

"Not like people then?" Magnus asked, with a sad smile, staring out at the dark afternoon.

Any hint of the sun was now completely hidden behind layers of thick, grey clouds. Several tendrils of mist and fog were forming and swirling on the forest floor. Sharp, cold air seeped in from outside and touched Magnus' face like a knife.

"You'd never feel lost if you believed you were right where you were meant to be."

"I don't know if I've ever felt that way." Magnus turned back to look at Matilda.

"Not even now?" Matilda's green eyes smiled at him.

"Today I feel—it's too much. Today I feel both lost and found." He tried to smile back, but his face felt like hard plastic. "You're here. But Glenn—."

Matilda walked to a corner of the room and bent to lift two pails of water. Magnus ran to help her. He lifted the pails and carried them to the stove, where he poured them on the fire. The coals sizzled as smoke and steam poured through the air.

"Now we're ready to go," Matilda said, half-hidden by the grey smog.

"To the doctor?"

"No. Amelia is taking care of Glenn. I'll take you home."

Magnus hesitated, crossed his arms in front of him and then dropped them to his sides.

"Where is that?"

"Home is the place we all want to be. The place everyone searches for."

Magnus felt his chest tighten. He was unsure if she meant Glenn's house, or if she was referring to the afterlife and that Glenn was going there. Or perhaps she meant that she was going to lead him out of the forest, back to his condo in the city. Because he was afraid of her answer, he did not ask her to clarify.

"Trust me," she said. "Glenn knows where his home is. One day, you will too."

The Easiest Communication

Matilda glided confidently through the mist, like she knew where to go without seeing the way. Magnus, lacking confidence even with perfect visibility, stuck close to her. Each exhalation of their breath was visible before them in the cold air, and then disappeared to swirl along with the mist.

"Amelia is your older self, isn't she?" Magnus blurted out.

"Yes. A possibility of myself."

"She's not as kind as you are." Magnus blushed. "Not to say—I mean—I'm sure you won't become like her. I mean—. I'm sorry. I mean you're very, very kind."

"You're mistaken to think one's older self is always better or kinder or wiser. She's loved Glenn a long time. While waiting for him, she became…prickly."

"Why haven't they married?" Magnus recalled how Glenn had touched Amelia's arm the day they first came to his house.

"Glenn never told her he loved her."

A drop of water dripped from a branch and splattered on

Matilda's head. Magnus touched her red hair to brush away the moisture. Afraid he was being too forward, he quickly took his hand from her and stuffed it into his pocket. From the corner of his eye, he peered at her, noting the drops of mist still beading her hair, and thinking that he could write an entire book of poems about her.

"Would she have married him if he had asked?" Magnus asked.

"She would have once. But now she's too independent." Matilda raised her small hands to her mouth, cupped them and blew on them to warm them.

Magnus imitated her action with his own hands, and then again peeked at her face, trying to read her expression. As he did so, he tripped over a tree root. He stumbled forward, but just managed to keep himself from falling.

They walked on in silence, as Magnus thought how he knew, like he had never known anything else in his entire life, that he did not want to die fifty years from now without having told Matilda that he loved her. But the thought of announcing this out loud, caused his heart to pound wildly and his mouth to grow dry. He felt slightly light-headed again, and the mist and red leaves of a maple tree began to spin around him.

Instead of speaking he cupped his hands in front of his mouth and blew on them again. He breathed in and out several times, until he felt steady on his feet and his head was clear, and then he dropped his arms to dangle at his sides. His pinkie finger grazed Matilda's green dress.

When they stepped over a protruding tree root that was half-hidden in the mist, he steadied Matilda by touching her shoulder or arm. She did not thank him, but also did not pull away. He took that as a good sign, for he knew that she didn't really need his help. He hoped his actions would hint of his love for her.

Then guilt clenched his gut as he realized he was feeling joy when Glenn was ill. Shame washed over him, eradicating his happiness.

She paused and pointed to the forest floor. Magnus looked down and saw a plump mouse.

"It's singing," she said. "Listen."

Magnus cocked his head and could just hear the high-pitched haunting call of the creature. It was almost outside the periphery of his ability to hear.

"Mice sing to each other to attract a mate," she said.

Magnus thought that it almost seemed that the mouse was serenading them.

They walked onward. As they climbed over a log, low laughter rolled out from behind a rotting stump to their left. Magnus kept walking, but the colour drained from his face. Again he peered at Matilda from the corner of his eyes. From what he could see, her face didn't change expression, so Magnus concluded she must not have heard the laughter.

Fool, fool, fool, a voice said, drifting towards him from the direction that the laughter had come.

Magnus stumbled as an intense pain shot through his knee and he cried out.

"My knee," he explained quickly. "It's still weak from the car accident."

Matilda said nothing, as she took his arm and steadied him. He took a few deep breaths, rubbed his knee and the pain disappeared again.

"We're almost at Glenn's house," she said.

Magnus nodded, realizing he had known all along that was where she was taking him, but he had hidden the knowledge from himself. He imagined Glenn saying: *You're not all that unusual. People hide the truth from themselves all the time.*

In his mind Magnus answered: *People are fools.*

Matilda walked lightly, sometimes on tiptoe, like any moment she would hover above the ground and fly alongside him. Hardly a branch or twig cracked under her steps.

The mist lifted for a few moments, and through the canopy of red maple leaves, Magnus noticed the enormity of the heavy grey sky. A dozen vultures circled overhead, black forms revealing themselves and then disappearing into the mist. They were like giant needles knitting the clouds into the heavens.

He felt how small he was in the expanse. Then peace descended on him, for as he took in the sky and the birds in it, he felt himself part of the entire world, and as part of it, he was as large. Goosebumps formed on his arms. He envied the birds, for he thought that they had the best perspective possible, seeing so much from above. He thought the vultures must know far more than they could say.

Glenn's voice echoed in his mind, and Magnus imagined him saying, *Our perspective from below is as good. From above or below, we are looking beyond our own narrow lives.*

Magnus agreed silently with Glenn. His hand again brushed against Matilda's dress, and this time just slightly touched her hand.

Neither Magnus nor Matilda spoke as they walked quickly onward, the mist swirling around them. Magnus felt no need to break open the silence with his words. To say anything now would have felt as disruptive as speaking during a symphony. The stillness between them felt like the gentlest, easiest communication Magnus had ever experienced.

Legends Of The Secret Bookstore

At Glenn's house, Amelia and Elliott sat on either side of Glenn's bed, while the raven perched on the window sill. Heat radiated from the fire in the hearth that Magnus presumed Amelia had made. A compress lay on Glenn's forehead. With each breath, his beard rose and fell on his chest. His face was pale and grey, coloured like the evening sky.

A bitter-smelling tea and a half-eaten bowl of soup rested on the table beside Glenn. Amelia's brow was furrowed and dark smudges circled her eyes. She looked even older than she had that morning. In contrast, although Glenn was clearly ill, his demeanor was tranquil and there was something about his expression that looked strikingly young, like Elliott.

Immediately, seeing Glenn so at peace, Magnus knew that he had to let him go. The grief squeezing his heart remained, but the inner agitation and fear disappeared.

When Magnus entered Glenn's bedroom, the raven flew from the window to Magnus' head and with its large beak tugged at a lock of his hair. They all laughed. For an instant Magnus felt guilty for the laughter. The next moment he realized it was appropriate; Glenn desired joy, especially now. The bird left his head and sat on the hook holding Glenn's bearskin coat. Magnus brushed a hand over his hair, smoothing it down, noting it was growing shaggy.

"Matilda," Glenn said. His voice was so weak that they all had to lean close to hear him. "Truly, you are as beautiful as I remembered. Welcome."

Matilda kissed his cheek.

"What if that book was the only one you ever got?" Glenn asked Magnus. He pointed with a shaky hand to Magnus' leather book that was on the table beside him. "Would you be content?"

"No." Magnus shook his head. He wondered if Glenn had been reading what he had written down through the journey. The raven flew from the bearskin coat to Amelia's shoulder. Its wings sounded like rustling silk in the small room.

"Good. Then you must keep searching for the bookstore. I'm giving you my house and the job of forest warden. While searching, please take care of the forest."

Magnus nodded because he wanted to make Glenn happy, but he did not want the house or the job. He wanted to find the bookstore, and return home to the city. His shoulders tightened at the thought of the extra burden of having to care for the forest.

"Why is the bookstore hidden?" Elliott asked suddenly.

"Well, there's a legend as to why The Secret Bookstore is here in this forest, and how it got started," Matilda said, sitting on the edge of Glenn's bed. Elliott approached her and she lifted him onto her lap.

Magnus sat on a chair beside Amelia. Their legs almost touched. The back of his head brushed the bearskin coat. He shuffled the chair forward a little, so his knees touched Glenn's bed. The walking stick was still leaning against the wall, and Magnus picked it up and held it tightly in both his hands, and bent towards Glenn.

There was little extra space in the small room, but even with all of them there it did not feel crowded. Instead Magnus felt a warm connection between the five of them.

"Once there was a husband and wife who together owned a bookstore with many rare books," Matilda said. "They contained ancient wisdom and secrets to the mysteries of life. The man and woman prided themselves on choosing the right book for anyone who came by asking for it."

"But how did they choose the right book?" Elliott asked, fidgeting with one of Matilda's glass bead necklaces.

"They both had a special gift, and they always just knew intuitively. Like you know which stone or pine cone to pick up," Matilda answered. "But people didn't buy enough books for them to make a living. Most people preferred watching the gladiators compete, a Greek comedy, a bullfight, horse racing or television. So they decided to give away the books. But when they gave them away, people did not value them. Instead they ripped them up to use as paper to start fires. Or they used them as stools to step on to reach things. Others took the books and sold them when they realized their monetary worth."

A piece of dry wood popped in the fire place. Everyone jumped.

Amelia stood slowly. Magnus could almost hear her joints creaking with age. She picked up a stick of wood from the pile beside the fireplace. Seeing how wearily she moved, Magnus leapt up, took the wood from her and shoved it and several more sticks into the fire.

Once Amelia and Magnus were seated again, Matilda continued: "The bookstore owners decided that they had to find a way to give the books to people who would appreciate them. The wife suggested moving into the desert, where only mystics and madmen lived. If people wanted a book, they would have to come to them. The cost would be the journey to find the book.

"The husband agreed that this sounded like a wise plan, so they loaded up nearly a dozen wagons with books and left the city. They made it as far as a forest, where the man died suddenly of a heart attack. The woman stopped there. She lived in the wagons with the books and took care of herself by using what the forest provided. When someone came who she believed was worthy of a book, she gave one away. When she grew old, she passed on the job of keeper of The Secret Bookstore to a friend, a wise young man, who lived in the forest.

"She asked him to follow three simple rules. First, each person was to receive only one book. Second, the owner should choose the book he thought suited that person. Third, the book could not be paid for. The man agreed. He was cautious; people were learning about the store, so to prevent theft, he took the books from the wagons and hid them in trees throughout the forest. He carefully followed her instructions. So the bookstore became hidden and secret."

"That's a good story," Glenn said. "But there is another legend. Please, tell it to us, Amelia."

Elliott jumped from Matilda's lap and moved as though to approach Amelia. Then he paused, thinking better of it as he saw her tired face and sharp eyes, and instead turned and sat on the edge of Glenn's bed beside Matilda.

"Before the creation of written language there lived a wise man," Amelia said. Her voice cracked, and she stopped speaking and cleared her throat. "This man lived for five hundred years. When he was three hundred years old, written language was developed. Then people came to him, asking him to write down what he said. But he would write nothing, except several lines in the sand that he would then wipe away with his feet."

Her voice cracked again. She wiped her brow with the

bottom of one of the layers of her skirts. As she lowered the skirt, she quickly wiped her cheeks as well. She sniffed and then covered over this sound by clearing her throat again. The raven echoed her, also making a guttural sound. Tears formed in Magnus' eyes, and he blinked them away, biting the inside of his cheek.

"Shall I tell the rest of the story?" Matilda asked. "I know it well."

"Go on," Amelia said, hoarsely.

"People came, listened to him, left and then wrote down what he said. His words and actions filled hundreds of books. When the man heard what people were doing, he was angry and stopped giving lectures. He did not believe he was wise. He merely thought he was observant. He wanted each person to discover their own wisdom."

"Stubborn fool," Glenn said.

"Being stubborn doesn't make one foolish," Amelia responded, clearing her throat and then staring at Glenn.

Magnus noted that her face was more tender than he had ever seen it. A lump formed in his throat. He pinched his finger nails into his palms so he wouldn't start sobbing there in front of everyone.

A long thin pause stretched out. Elliott shifted restlessly on the bed. Magnus imagined the tangled red ball of yarn flying through the room, tying them all together.

"What happened next?" Elliott asked at last.

Magnus' shoulders relaxed.

"The man spent the next two hundred years looking for and gathering every book written about him," Matilda continued. "He did not destroy them for he recognized them as beautiful creations worthy of existence. Instead he hid them away. But his job never ended. Even as he found one book, many more were being created."

"How many?" Elliott asked, his eyes wide. He bounced on the bed.

"Thousands. Maybe millions. As he was dying, his two daughters begged him to give them permission to give away books to true seekers, those who sincerely needed them. That way, no one would take monetary profit from his wisdom. They argued that what people did with the books was not his responsibility. Just before he died, he finally agreed to their request. Because there were many attempts to steal them, the daughters hid them throughout the world—in caves, tree hollows, locked rooms in castles and clay pots in desert sands. Each book was only to be given away to those who were deemed worthy."

Magnus asked Elliott, "Which story do you think is true?"

"Both," he exclaimed, joyfully throwing his arms up into the air.

"Of course," Glenn said. "Why not? Stories of all kinds encompass much truth, just like The Secret Bookstore."

A sudden coughing fit seized Glenn. He held a handkerchief to his mouth. A few drops of blood were on it when he took it away.

The Young Rich Man

A knock at the door startled them all. While Magnus went to answer the door, blinking away tears, Matilda took Elliott to the kitchen for something to eat and drink.

Magnus opened the door. A young man in his twenties with sallow skin and several days' growth of beard stood there, clutching maps in his hands. His bicycle leaned against him, loaded with suitcases and backpacks and canvas sacks. After he said that he sought The Secret Bookstore, showing a business card with its name, Magnus invited him into the kitchen. Matilda gave him a mug of coffee and a thick slice of Amelia's homemade bread and strawberry jam.

"Why are you looking for the bookstore?" Magnus asked.

The man pushed away from the table and stood up.

"Everything in my life has been easy," he said. He took off his cap and twisted it in his hands. "I inherited money. I did well in school. I have lots of friends and a beautiful family. But to what purpose? What's the meaning of it all? There's no challenge left, except to earn more money or spend more money. No, there must be something more, something I should be doing.

"One evening I was out walking and thinking, and a complete stranger, a kind man, gave me this card and said I could find the answers I wanted in a book at The Secret Bookstore. My wife told me I should go, for I'd never be satisfied otherwise. I've been searching for two years."

Magnus kept himself in check, but wanted to shout: *Two years!* He couldn't imagine wandering the forest for years. Neither the man, nor Elliott, nor Matilda seemed to have noticed his shock; he had managed to keep his face blank like an expert poker player.

"Then why don't you just give everything away?" Elliott said, passing the man a handful of acorns from his pail.

The man tilted his head and scratched his brow with his cap, as though considering Elliott's words.

"Sounds easy," the man said. "Just like that. No one ever suggested that before."

"Sure. See? Here you go." Elliott gave him some more acorns. Then he pulled out a brown snake, about the length of his arm.

"Do you want him? I call him Bob," Elliott said. "He's a beauty."

The young man jerked backwards and said, "No thanks."

Magnus started to laugh, but stopped when he saw the

disappointment on the boy's face.

"The acorns are enough," the young man added. "Thanks."

"How about a caterpillar?" Elliott asked. His face brightened again. "A yellow one? Robin thinks you'd like that much better."

"Who's Robin?" the man asked.

"My best friend. Here, don't you see him?" Elliott pointed into the empty space beside him.

The man smiled stiffly and twirled the cap in his hands. Elliott put the snake back in the pail and took out the promised yellow caterpillar.

"Thank you. This is plenty," the young man said, taking the caterpillar. The yellow caterpillar curled up into a protective ball in his hand. "You're very generous."

"That was very kind of you," Matilda said to Elliott, who beamed in response.

Magnus left the man, Elliott and Matilda in the kitchen. He went to Glenn and told him about the man seeking the bookstore. Amelia sat on a chair in the corner, silently listening.

"What should I do for him?" Magnus asked. "I don't know where to send him or how to help. But I'd like to do something. He's been searching for two years. Two years!"

"Do the same thing you did for the elderly couple," Glenn whispered. "Sit on the throne outside your bedroom window and look into his heart. Then pick one book for him from my shelves. Let him read that while he continues looking for The

Secret Bookstore."

"I didn't think it would be this hard to find a bookstore," Magnus said, and heaved a heavy sigh. He shook his head, perplexed. "Two years! If he hasn't found it in all this time, how will I ever find it when you're gone?"

"You're mistaken," Glenn said, faintly. "I'm dying, but not leaving. I've taught you all you will need to know to find it. Trust me. Two days or two years doesn't matter. Time isn't real."

Magnus doubted Glenn's words. Aloud, he said, "I'm trying to trust, truly."

Magnus sat on the stump outside, closed his eyes and remembered the vulture's silent flight. Magnus sensed that the rich young man's soul was deep blue, and heavy with many cares. As he imagined the bookshelves, Magnus felt his own heart stir, as if it were speaking to him with pictures. His heart showed him the smallest book on the shelf, something that just fit in the palm of his hand. He thought that felt appropriate—he'd give the man something light that would not weigh him down for he already carried so much.

Magnus opened his eyes and went to the bookshelves. A bright light darted across the small book he had just envisioned.

Magnus smiled faintly, as he scribbled a poem on the back of the book jacket for the young man:

Do You Prefer the Cultivated Mind or the Wild One?

If I were poor,
I'd pick You
a bouquet of wildflowers.

If I were rich,
I'd pick You
a bouquet of wild flowers
and paint them

gold.

Magnus then sent the young man away to continue looking for The Secret Bookstore. The young man left behind his bicycle and bags and maps, his face pressed into the back page of the book, where Magnus had written the poem. He ignored Magnus when Magnus called after him that he'd forgotten his bike and bags. After he shouted to the rich young man several times, Matilda put a hand on Magnus' arm. Magnus stopped calling, letting him keep walking away, each of his steps crunching over dried leaves.

Seeing the young man so deeply immersed in the poem he had written and listening to his footsteps fade away, Magnus felt peaceful, sensing somehow that he had done something good for the young man.

Suddenly, Magnus heard another poem rising in him. It would be about always hearing his own footsteps on gravel, grass, leaves, pine needles—as long as two things were done. First, he must listen. Second, he must keep walking.

Love

"I think that young man is going to start getting rid of everything he doesn't need," Magnus told Glenn.

He then glanced through the bedroom window, and saw Amelia outside sitting on the woodpile. A square of sunlight poured through the tree tops and rested on her. Her head leaning back and resting on a piece of wood, she looked small and fragile.

He bent close to Glenn. He knew that he had to speak now, while Amelia wasn't here. "Do you love Amelia?" Magnus asked, his voice low, just above a whisper.

"Yes." Glenn looked down at his hand folded on top of his blankets.

"Did you ever tell her?"

"I was a shy young man. Then a shy slightly older man. Days became years. At some point, it seemed too late and better to leave things as they were. She was always telling me that she was too much older than me. I thought she meant it."

"Why didn't you sit out on your wooden throne and look into her heart?"

"I'm not all that wise," Glenn said. He unfolded his hands and fidgeted with the end of his long beard. His calloused hands still looked strong, even near death.

"You are wise. But you were also afraid." Magnus was surprised at his sudden understanding that Glenn had flaws, just like any human.

"Yes. Fear makes people foolish."

"I'm afraid of not finding my purpose, of not finding the store, of losing you," Magnus said. "Terrified. Confused about this entire journey."

"I remember feeling that way once," Glenn said.

Magnus hesitated, and then leaned even closer to Glenn. A sudden pattering above their heads startled him.

"Squirrels on the roof," Glenn said, with a slight chuckle.

The chuckle led to a fit of coughing. Once Glenn stopped coughing and was relatively comfortable, Magnus glanced at the doorway to make sure no one was there.

"Do you think Matilda loves me?" he whispered, looking back at Glenn.

"I don't know."

"I have to tell her I love her, don't I?"

"That would be wise." Glenn smiled again.

"But, wait!" Magnus exclaimed, and sprung up. "If there's no time, like you've told me over and over, then it's not too late to tell Amelia. Nothing could ever be too late or too early."

"I don't think now—."

"If I can learn from Elliott, why can't you learn from me?" Magnus asked.

Glenn paused for a long time before answering: "It's unexpected."

"You taught me what I'm telling you," Magnus said.

"And that's how I know I can leave," Glenn said. "You have your own wisdom now. And it will grow best without me here. There comes a point when the teacher is a hindrance."

"Then stay and learn from me."

"Was I ever as bold and pushy as you?" Glenn asked.

"You still are."

They chuckled together. Glenn stopped laughing abruptly and took Magnus' hand in his own weak one.

"I want to become a tree," Glenn said. "Let me stand for a hundred years with all these other trees. Alone, but never alone. They lean back and forth, and their branches touch briefly. The roots entwine. But the trunks are separate. So they are many, and they are one. So I am one, I am many. You understand?"

"Yes," Magnus said. "I promise."

Someone knocked at the bedroom door. A second later Amelia entered. Her eyes were as sharp as glass flowers with broken edges.

"This man wants to talk to you," Magnus said to Amelia.

He left the room to leave Glenn and Amelia alone together.

Saying Goodbye

Early that afternoon Glenn shuddered like a leaf on a tree, rattled by an autumn wind.

Then he was gone.

Magnus buried Glenn's body in the forest, under an oak tree. Elliott planned to place his misshapen paper birthday hat on the grave, but at the last minute, he changed his mind. Instead he put the hat back on, and he and Matilda made a bouquet of wild flowers and twigs and placed this on the grave. Around the bouquet Elliott placed several of his favourite rocks, acorns and black walnuts. He looked at it for a long time. Then he decided it needed one more thing, and added a black and orange caterpillar.

Magnus wrote a poem in his journal. He ripped out the paper and pierced the page with a stick and pressed the stick into the ground as a temporary memorial.

Back in Time

a murderous wind
  rattles
the forest

dry leaves clatter
and clap

one hurls
itself
from a branch,
                    jousts
with death

another
  spins
          floats
     drifts
through
      the death
  waltz

both reach
that common
      dusty destination
where all are
born

into (no) time

tight buds
unfurl
sung back
home

by peeper frogs

He ripped out a second piece of paper and wrote down *Glenn The Magnificent* and then pierced that with another stick and also pushed that into the ground beside the poem.

Magnus knew that the sun, rain and wind would slowly cause the papers to disintegrate and scatter. Then there'd be no trace of where Glenn had been buried, just as Glenn wanted.

Amelia wept. Her eyes were shattered glass. When she stopped crying, her hand shook as she pointed at Glenn's grave.

"Bury me beside him when I die," she said.

The raven, standing on a nearby maple tree, cawed and spread out its wings. Magnus shivered at the mournful sound. Amelia reached out and took Magnus' arm, and leaned on him, using him as if he were a walking stick. Magnus glanced back. A fox stood at Glenn's graveside looking back directly at Magnus. Tears choked him, but he didn't cry. When Amelia turned to see what Magnus was looking at, the fox trotted away into the woods.

As Magnus helped Amelia walk back to Glenn's house, the

raven flew from tree to tree alongside them. Magnus looked back again to see if Matilda was following them, but she had disappeared into the forest as quickly and quietly as the fox.

As he felt the depth of her absence, his knee gave out. Magnus stumbled to the ground. Amelia half-fell with him, but she managed to remain upright. He pushed his hands against the ground and stood again. Several pine needles from the ground stuck into his palms. He yanked them out and dropped them to the forest floor. One had pierced his skin and drawn a drop of blood. Magnus wiped his hand on his pants, trying to ignore the pain in his hand and in his heart.

Remembering how Glenn had not told Amelia of his love, when they were young, Magnus knew he could not waste a moment. He ran back to tell Matilda that he loved her. He just caught a glimpse of red hair disappearing into a group of pine trees. When he ran to the pines, he found no trace of her.

Suddenly, a downy woodpecker hammered a tree nearby. Its rhythmic drumming echoed through the forest. It hopped a few feet down the tree trunk, and then clung to the tree with its strong hooked claws and pounded the tree again.

"A lonely sound," Amelia said, standing close beside him.

Forcing down tears, Magnus whispered: "Will I ever see her again?"

"I don't know."

Magnus let Amelia take his arm. They continued walking forward, more slowly this time.

Magnus wondered what she and Glenn had spoken about before he died. He hoped Glenn had told her at last of his love for her.

He felt a new poem arise inside of him:

Omniscient

I know
love as
woodpeckers know
trees

I know love, like
the soul knows
the body

I know
nothing
like love knows

the heat of glowing coals
in my heart

The Second Goodbye

A week after Glenn's death, Magnus and Elliott built a fort out of twigs and branches that they had heaped up against a boulder. They gathered piles of dried leaves and armfuls of moss to make a soft floor.

"Glenn would like this fort," Elliott said. "He'd love how big it is."

Since Glenn's death, Elliott had talked non-stop about him. Although remembering Glenn caused his throat to tighten and his heart to ache, Magnus realized it was helpful for Elliott, so he encouraged the reminiscing. Sometimes it even felt as if Glenn were nearby, eavesdropping, the memory of him was so tangible.

Matilda's absence hurt him too. After her disappearance at Glenn's grave, she had not returned. Amelia claimed not to know where Matilda lived. Magnus had wandered around the forest with Elliott, trying to find Matilda's cabin again, but he had not succeeded.

Now Magnus left Elliott to go a short distance away to pick up a long branch for the roof of the fort. When he turned back, he saw a tall woman walking briskly towards them. She wore high heels, black dress pants and a silver blouse.

"Mom!" Elliot yelled.

Leaves scattered as he ran to her. They embraced.

"It's time to return home and start school," she said.

"I don't want to go," said Elliott, stomping a foot. Several maple leaves fluttered up into the air. "I like it here."

"Don't you want to be a big boy and learn to read and write?" his mother asked.

Elliott looked from his mother back to Magnus. Magnus shrugged at Elliott, as if to say that he couldn't stop Elliott's mother from taking him back. She did not see Magnus, for he kept himself hidden from her by remaining behind several large bushes.

He had not looked at photos of his mother for many years, and had forgotten how beautiful she once had been. The mother he remembered had been much heavier, her hair short and grey, her thin lips always pursed and her eyes squinted in disapproval.

"Of course you do. You're not a baby anymore."

She plucked a twig from Elliott's hair and brushed leaves from his back. She took one of his hands, and shook her head as she appraised his ragged fingernails.

Magnus glanced at his own hands. His nails were as dirty as

Elliott's. He ran a hand over his hair and smoothed his beard and felt bits of dried leaves in both. He probably looked as dishevelled as Elliott. He had given little consideration to his appearance since he'd left the city. By now he must look like a wild vagabond.

"You'll need a long bath when you get home," Elliott's mom said.

"I hate baths," Elliott said. "Here in the forest, it's always too hot or too cold. We add too much or not enough boiling water."

The woman's face resembled porcelain, unimpressed by Elliott's excuses.

"It is fortunate I came when I did," his mother said, in a clipped voice, each of her words carefully enunciated. "If I had have come later, you'd be so wild that it would have taken weeks to get you back into a normal routine."

Elliott whispered to Robin.

"Please don't do that," his mother said. "The children at school will laugh at you for talking to an imaginary person. Do you want them to laugh at you?"

"No," Elliott said. "But he's not imaginary. Robin is just invisible. He wants you to listen to him."

His mother tugged at Elliott's jacket so he would stand up straight. He squirmed, but didn't make a sound.

As Magnus observed Elliott's mother teaching him to be afraid of what other people thought about him, he curled his toes inside his shoes to keep himself from trying to stop her. In the next moment, Magnus realized that although it was Elliott's mother who was chasing Robin away, if it had not been her, it would have been another adult. Then he understood that if it had not been himself that had taught Elliott to sink through the water, it would have been someone else.

Magnus knew that in moment after moment like this, the boy would gradually leave his own life. He would clothe himself in layer upon layer of disguises. He'd accumulate fears and insecurities and try not to reveal that he had them, until one day Elliott wouldn't know who he was. He would wake up on a firm mattress in the city. And each day he would put on a suit and tie, and go to his office. He would not know his purpose, or what he liked or hated or was naturally good at because he had spent most of his life assimilating. He would forget what it felt like to splash in puddles. He would stop believing in fairy tales. He would buy a sports car and a power suit to try make him feel authoritative and important.

Finally, when he was thirty-three, spurred on by seven vultures and a mouse, he would doubt himself— and try to return to the self he had once been as a seven-year-old boy.

Panic rushed over Magnus as he wondered how he could keep this child from further losing himself. Perhaps, if he saved Elliott, he would change everything for himself in the present. He wanted to convince his mother to leave Elliott with him. But he hesitated. He doubted that he would be a better role model for the boy.

And rightfully, a child belonged with his parents. Magnus feared that he couldn't take care of the child without Glenn's help. But he wasn't ready to let Elliott go. He half-rose from his place behind the bushes to approach Elliott and his mother.

But then he remembered a lesson Glenn had shared on their journey. Glenn believed that people, animals and things remained in one's life for as long as they were needed. Not a moment longer. Magnus wondered if because Elliott was leaving, the boy was no longer needed in his life; and, if at some level, Elliott no longer needed him. Surely, that was why his mother had arrived now. Magnus crouched down again.

Elliott picked up his crumpled birthday hat and his pail, which held several stones and pinecones and a red maple leaf as large as his head.

"We have to hurry now," his mother said.

She took Elliott's arm in her hand, causing him to drop his birthday hat. He reached back to pick it up, but she marched him quickly forward. Elliott stumbled beside her. Then he ripped his arm away from her and ran back to the hat. He picked it up and defiantly stuck it on his head. His mother followed him, grabbed his hand and pulled the hat off again.

"It's a disgusting, dirty old thing," she said.

She tossed the shapeless hat back on the forest floor. Elliott's face fell, but his mother marched onward. Magnus felt as if he had betrayed the boy, but did not stop him from leaving.

"Wait," Elliott cried. "Please, I see a snake. It's a beauty."

His mother screamed and started to run, still tightly clutching Elliott's hand. He stumbled beside her, trying to keep up.

Magnus scrambled up a tree. Elliott had taught him how to climb, and now that he had lost weight and gained muscle, he was more agile than he'd been in years. His knee was much stronger and gave him less trouble than it had at the start of the journey.

He silently wept as he watched Elliott and his mother disappear through the trees.

He had lost both his future and his past. He wondered what he had left.

As much as he had worried how he'd care for the boy, he now worried how he'd live there all alone. He glanced up. A single vulture circled overhead. He had never felt so lonely.

A Man Called Blue

That evening, a short man with a square face knocked on the door of Glenn's house. Although Magnus did not feel like socializing, and wanted to hide in the house and pretend no one was home, he forced himself to go out and meet the man and invite him inside.

The man kept tugging at his blue suspenders. Someone had sewn the suspenders to his bottle-green pants with large stitches of yellow yarn. Both his pants and suspenders looked homemade.

"Can I help you?" Magnus asked, as he folded his arms across his chest.

"I don't rightly know," the man answered. "I told myself I was going to go for a long walk this morning. And then I thought I might walk on to my daughter's house. Now I'm here."

"Are you lost?"

"Not really. Just meandering. I found this business card on

the ground at the end of my driveway."

He held out the card, so Magnus could read the words: *The Secret Bookstore*. He led the short man through the house to the living room with the bookshelves. He saw a light dancing on the spine of a red book. Magnus plucked the book from the shelf and gave it to him.

"I'm sorry. But there's something wrong here," the man said, his voice gruff. He loudly snapped his suspenders.

Magnus peered over the man's shoulder. The man pointed at one of Magnus' favourite poems that he had written on a blank page at the front of the book. Magnus wondered if his handwriting was too messy to read.

"It doesn't rhyme," the man grumbled. He read the poem aloud:

Abandoned Graveyard

a snake
  slides
     amongst
tall   grass

a stray wind
     whistles
    through
a window   screen

an old man's cough
    echoes
in   the empty kitchen
the nearly tangible
   voices
remains   of my soul

"See. Nothing rhymes."

"No," Magnus said, trying to keep the irritation out of his voice. "It doesn't." He wanted the man to go away, and leave him alone with his grief.

"That's not a real poem. Poems should rhyme."

"It's modern. I don't write rhyming poetry," Magnus explained, doing his best to remain civil, but his voice was sharp.

"Do you have something else? I don't read poetry. I don't understand it. I can't do anything with this."

Magnus sighed. He did not know why he cared, but he felt sad that this man did not like his poem. He wondered what Glenn would do. Then he speculated about what Elliott would have done. And finally, he considered the possible responses of Matilda and Amelia. None of them would have sent the man away empty-handed. He believed that if the four of them had had a discussion about it, they would have suggested that Magnus offer the man a true story, and the only story he had inside him right now was about his journey thus far.

"What's your name?" Magnus asked.

"People call me Blue." The man paused. "It's the blue suspenders. My mom made blue ones for me when I was a boy. I wouldn't go anywhere without them. Since then I've always worn blue suspenders. I made this pair myself out of my wife's leather purse after she died last year."

"Have a seat," Magnus said, gesturing at an armchair.

Blue sat down. Magnus paced from one end of the living room to the other as he described the turkey vultures that sat on top of his Porsche, and the mouse inside of it. He explained how he had followed Glenn here, looking for his purpose, and found Elliott on the way. And then he described losing Glenn, Elliott, and Matilda within a short time. All he had left was Amelia and himself.

Magnus had to stop speaking several times as he wept. Blue waited silently while Magnus blew his nose in a handkerchief, dried his eyes and continued. The losses seemed to deepen as Magnus spoke of them, but he continued talking until he arrived at the end of the story.

"And here you are," Magnus said. "Blue. A man who does not like poetry."

"That is some story," Blue said.

Magnus picked up the book that he had given Blue, and scribbled another poem on the inside of the back cover:

Found

if the map was blank
as a cloudy midnight sky

I'd throw a red feather
into the air

and go the way it points

planning to get lost
on a dusty dirt road

Blue read the new poem.

"I still don't understand. A blank map? Why not just use a compass? Why throw the feather into the air? I'd prefer a newspaper article. But I'll take the book and give it to my daughter. She'll like it. She talks like you write, and so we always end up arguing."

Magnus knew, without knowing how he knew, that Blue had not spoken to his daughter for a very long time. He sensed this poem might be used to start a reconciliation.

He offered Blue a place to stay for the night, but the man insisted on going home, even though it was growing dark and wolves howled in the distance. Blue said he would be fine. He took a flashlight out of his jacket pocket, flicked it on and walked away through the trees.

Magnus closed the door and went to bed, where he tossed and turned for hours. Finally, he got up and sat outside on the wooden throne under his bedroom window. The wolves had stopped howling. He heard the tiny squeaks of bats, as they flew around the house catching insects. Their high-pitched peeps comforted him, for he wanted the nearby presence of some living creature.

Finally, just before dawn, still seated on the stump, wrapped in a woolen blanket, Magnus' headed nodded and he fell into a restless sleep.

Alone

The day after Elliott left, Magnus tried to leave behind his grief and loneliness by completely focusing his mind on looking for the bookstore and Matilda.

He decided he would try to cross the river that passed Amelia's house. However, once he was there and he stood near the water, he shook and broke out in a cold sweat. He forced himself to ignore his pounding heart and put a foot out onto the water. It sank through. He yanked it back out.

Then he walked along the river, hoping to find a bridge or a narrow section he could jump across. He was frustrated, but not surprised, when he found neither.

Frequently, that day he peered up through the tree branches and leaves to the sky for vultures. Each time, he was disappointed at their absence. Glenn had said they'd leave and find warmer climates for the winter, but Magnus had not believed him. Now he realized that he had grown accustomed to the vultures that he had once loathed and feared. Without them, the sky looked desolate and empty, the world seemed too vast, and he felt alone.

He did not return to Glenn's home until dark that evening. Back inside the house, he took the walking stick from Glenn's room, still leaning against the wall at the head of his bed, and placed it in a corner of his own bedroom, beside his own walking stick.

Before going to bed he scribbled a poem in his journal:

Lighter Burdens

As you walk,
carry bags of poems
or gold coins
or magic beans
or horse manure
or wild grapes
or willow branches
or glass beads
or clods of earth
or toads
or walking sticks.

Their weight on your back,
know the currency
you claim.

The two sticks, side by side, were the last things he saw before he fell asleep.

The next day he didn't go near the river. Instead he wandered the forest, hoping some clue would appear to reveal the bookstore to him. Instead he found another tree that had been cut down by the trespasser. He read a note nailed to it: *I'm looking for the bookstore. All the books will be mine.*

As he read it, Magnus heard a voice say: *Fool.*

He saw a shadowy figure to his left. Ignoring the sharp pain in his knee, he turned and ran several steps after it through the forest, before being stopped by thick bushes with long thorns. He peered through the undergrowth and saw no one. Although he shook with fear, and kept jumping at shadows and twigs snapping under his feet, he forced himself to continue walking and searching for the store.

Day after day, Magnus went out looking for the bookstore. Some days he returned to the river and made another attempt at walking across it or finding a bridge. Other days he meandered through the forest.

Several times he went to Amelia's and visited with her briefly, but found little comfort in her acerbic presence. He found no more cut-down trees, no stray travelers looking for the bookstore, and didn't hear the low voice or see the elusive shadow.

In the middle of November he woke up to the first falling snowflakes. The sound of them ticking like a clock against his bedroom window was the loneliest sound he had ever heard. A single sparrow shivered at the foot of a white pine tree. Magnus thought of how Elliott would have wanted to catch it and keep it warm inside. A rising wind whistled through the trees and caused the upper branches to wave wildly. Magnus imagined they were telling him goodbye, encouraging him to leave.

He thought that he had been foolish to think he could find the bookstore or the man cutting down the trees without the help of Glenn or Elliott. He might have felt trapped in the city and his life as an accountant, but he had felt safe there. In his old life he had a variety of food, and television to watch, and people to talk to. It was not perfect, but, as he remembered it, it seemed better than this secluded home in a desolate snowy forest.

"Good idea," he said aloud to the waving trees. "I'm going home."

The Way Home

After breakfast, Magnus dressed in Glenn's boots, bearskin coat, deerskin gloves and pants and a woolen hat. He had lost so much weight since leaving the city, that they all fit him perfectly. His body had become thin and wiry, like Glenn's. He tucked his leather book inside the heavy coat. He left his walking stick beside Glenn's, feeling they should stay side by side, and that if he needed a stick, he'd find a tree branch.

Then he went to say goodbye to Amelia. She wasn't home, so he took a final look at her Gothic house and turned and walked the way he thought Glenn had taken when they entered.

He told himself that he looked forward to returning to the city— to a hot shower, a meal in a nice restaurant, his own bed, sidewalks filled with people, and grocery stores. He imagined that he would not miss Glenn's home, the smell of pine trees, the chopping of wood and building of fires.

Even though these were lies, he took comfort in thinking them.

His physical endurance had grown since he left the city, but even so, as he trudged through the steadily accumulating snow his legs grew rubbery with fatigue. Cold nibbled at his toes and fingers. Snow crusted his hat. He lost feeling in his cheeks.

Plodding onwards, he complained to the trees. Their hieroglyphics hadn't helped him find the location of The Secret Bookstore, or explained his true purpose. He spoke to the absent vultures, wishing they had never sat on his car. He accused them of chasing him out of the city by constantly circling him.

He spoke to the spirit of Glenn, asking him why he had brought him to this forest and then died and abandoned him. He was angry at Elliott's mother for taking the boy home. When he tripped over tree roots, fallen branches or stumps hidden under the snow, he yelled at them. He shouted loudly at the rock against which he he'd hit his knee. He was furious with himself for talking aloud to these things that didn't answer him. As he grumbled, argued, and raged, Magnus forgot his grief.

But when he suddenly paused and realized that he was lost, all his anger changed into fear. The heavy snowfall had erased his footprints, so he could not follow them back. He didn't know which way to go, but he knew that if he didn't find his way out of the forest and to shelter, or back to Glenn's, he could die in the snowstorm.

His chest tightened and throat constricted. He didn't want to die. Not like this. Not yet. He wasn't ready. He hadn't found his purpose. He hadn't walked on water. He hadn't told Matilda that he loved her. Now the terror of dying before he had accomplished these things, kept him walking onwards.

Magnus prayed for a sign to show him the way back to the city. Magnus prayed to run into Amelia or Matilda or a turkey vulture or any other wild animal. But instead of a symbolic sign, Magnus saw a wooden one.

A tall man with muscles bulging through his short-sleeved shirt was hammering a stick into the ground. Attached to the top of the stick was a sign with painted words: *The Way Home.* Beneath the words was an arrow pointing in the direction Magnus had been headed.

"Where are you going?" the man asked.

His head was shaved bald, but he didn't seem the least bit disturbed by the cold or snow melting on his bare scalp. Several large flakes had caught in his bushy black eyebrows and mustache.

Magnus attempted to speak, but his teeth chattered instead. He pointed at the sign.

"Home? Me too. What a coincidence. We'll travel together," the man said.

"But whose home?" Magnus asked, managing to stop chattering. "Yours or mine?"

"There's only one way home," the bald man said.

"You mean—d-d-death?"

Magnus clenched his teeth together to stop chattering. If he died alone here in the forest, no one would ever find him or know what had become of him. Or worse, no one would even wonder what happened to him. He realized the thought was self-pitying, but he wanted someone to miss him.

"No. There's only one way home," the man repeated.

He picked up the sledgehammer and swung it over his massive shoulder.

"I want to go back to my old home and life," Magnus said. "I'm going back to the city."

"Great. Me too. This is the way." The man started walking in the direction the sign pointed.

"Wait," Magnus called. "Who told you to put up the sign? How do you know the way?"

The man continued walking and without looking back, he said, "I decided to put it up because it's the way home. I entered the forest by myself, and I'll take myself out the same way. Everyone who sees it will know they want to go home too. They'll follow us."

Although he did not like or trust the man, to Magnus it seemed preferable to travel with someone than to go on alone. He did not mind being lost, as long as someone else walked with him.

As they plodded on, the muscular man said that he had also been looking for the bookstore.

"I've been looking for twenty years, and haven't ever seen a hint of it," he said. "I've searched the forest and its surroundings section by section. I've made maps of each area."

He showed Magnus a glimpse of a paper that he called a map. It was only a blank page. He shoved the paper back in his pocket. Magnus' stomach sank, and the hair on the back of his neck stood on end.

"What kind of book were you looking for?" he asked.

"A book for my boss. Someone gave my boss a business card and told him he could find a book about the Midas touch—how to turn anything he wanted into gold."

"Really?" Magnus said. "Who gave him the card?"

The bald man ignored his question. "My boss didn't want to give up his career or leave behind his family for years while he looked, so he hired me."

"But who gave him this card? Don't you think that only the person who receives the card can find the bookstore?" Magnus asked. "Doesn't each person have to go on the journey themselves?"

Instead of answering, the man strode away so quickly that Magnus could not keep up.

"Please slow down," Magnus shouted. The prospect of continuing on alone through the snowstorm terrified him.

"I'm in a hurry. If you can't keep up, that's your problem," the man said.

Magnus continued on the same route, stepping into the bald man's footprints, because it was easier than making his own tracks through the snow.

The Wolf

Magnus marched through the snowstorm, feeling more alone than at any other time in his life. The muscular man who had put up the sign had left him far behind. The snow beating against him felt like a foe. The eerie sound of a grey owl swooshing past startled him, causing him to trip over an invisible tree root and fall to the ground. With great effort, he stood upright again, as a bitter wind blasted directly into his face. The tree limbs weighed down by snow provided no shelter from the storm.

He walked on, and yearned to return to the city and his familiar life there. He visualized himself walking on the sidewalk with other people. But as he imagined this, he did not feel less lonely. He didn't miss anyone from his old life. He only missed the ability to numb himself with work.

He didn't want to return to that life. But he did not know how to live here in his new one.

"I belong nowhere now," he shouted aloud, terrified at the thought.

He picked up a handful of snow and hurled it at a nearby oak tree. A gust of wind blew it back into his face. He spun around. His head hit a branch, sending more snow cascading to the ground and onto his head. He kicked at the snow, angry that it didn't fight back. With a gloved fist, he pounded the oak tree.

"I will not die alone here in a snowstorm!" he shouted over and over.

The oak ignored him.

Finally, panting from exhaustion, he fell to the ground. He wanted to sob, but was afraid that if he started he would never stop. A voice inside said that if he stopped walking now, he'd freeze to death.

Nearby something moved. From behind a maple tree strode a grey wolf. As Magnus inched his way into a standing position, the wolf circled him. Step by step the wolf neared. It came so close that even in the dark, Magnus could see its glittering yellow eyes.

He tried to remember if Glenn had told him what to do if he saw a wolf. He didn't know if he should run, yell or stay still. Paralyzed with fear, he remained immobile. The wolf darted forward, grabbed his right hand, pulled off his glove and let the glove fall to the snow. Then the wolf took Magnus' bare hand in its powerful teeth and tugged. Magnus was surprised at its gentleness, and leaned forward to pet it.

Suddenly, he felt himself wake up, and realized the animal

might be gentle, but it was a wild beast and he yelled, "Hey!"

The wolf leapt backwards, lowered its head and wagged its tail. It covered its teeth with its lips and its tongue lolled out. However, the wolf didn't move back towards him. After a moment of hesitation, Magnus picked up his glove and put it on and walked away. He looked behind him, but the wolf didn't follow. After a moment, it disappeared from sight in the falling snow.

All Magnus' fears faded as he continued walking, for soon he was too exhausted to feel anything at all.

The Cabin Of Music

Magnus thought he heard music through the sound of falling snow. He paused, wondering if he was hallucinating. Seeing no better option, he plodded towards the music, hoping it was real.

The snow fell less furiously now, so he could see a few feet in front of him. The music grew louder, and an orange glow of light shone through the darkness. With a few more steps, Magnus could just see a log cabin. It spilled over with loud voices and laughter. A wolf with bared teeth stood at the doorway, watching him, as though it had been waiting for him to arrive.

Magnus stopped dead, and his blood roared in his ears as he inched backwards. Behind the wolf, the door opened and a boy ran out past the animal. The child tripped and sprawled in the deep snow. When he heard the boy laugh, Magnus knew it was Elliott, and tried to find a reserve of strength to run to him. However, he could do no more than plod onward. Still lying in the snow, Elliott moved his arms and legs, and shouted that he was making a snow angel.

When Magnus reached the boy, Elliott leapt up and hugged him. He wore a winter coat over pajamas. Instead of boots he wore furry dragon slippers.

"Magnus! You look like Glenn. You look like an old man!" Elliott exclaimed.

Magnus felt his beard with his gloved hand and pulled away snow and ice. He brushed snow from his eyebrows. He took off his snow-crusted hat. He knocked it against his knee and put it back on.

As Elliott started walking to the building, Magnus grabbed him.

"There's a wolf at the door," Magnus said.

"Don't worry. It's almost tame," Elliott answered.

"Almost?"

"Matilda told me we don't want to tame anything completely because then it would be dead. Things need a little wildness inside to stay alive. She says that's why grown-ups are all so boring. She says most of them have been tamed and there's not much life left in them."

"Do you think I'm boring?" Magnus tried to laugh, but he was so tired that he only half-grunted.

"Not as boring as you used to be," Elliott said. "Robin agrees with me. He says you're almost interesting now."

Giggling, Elliott darted away from Magnus, ran to the wolf, patted its head and opened the door. The wolf slipped inside behind the boy. Magnus hesitated at the door, but the promise of warmth drew him to risk moving by the animal, and he stumbled inside. Immediately, two more wolves joined the first one. The three wolves stood at the entranceway and stared silently at Magnus with their glittering yellow eyes.

Magnus tried to ignore them, and surveyed the single room. Each of the four walls had a fireplace with a roaring fire. The wall space around the north fireplace was lined with mirrors, reflecting the light from the oil lamps on the dozen tables scattered through the room. The mirrors made the one-room building look far larger than it was.

Magnus' heart leapt when he saw Matilda in one corner playing the fiddle, her red hair flying from side to side. Magnus wondered if her wildness, the part of her that remained untamed, was part of the reason that he loved her. Beside Matilda a man played the bones of an animal, rhythmically clacking them against each other. The bald man with bulging muscles, stood nearby with his sledgehammer over his shoulder, talking loudly to a short, stocky man beside him. Several couples danced around the room, and several others were seated and eating and drinking at the tables.

The entire room glowed with light, laughter, music and warmth, but Magnus' attention was drawn back to the wolves sitting at the doorway, who guarded both the way in and the way out.

His fingers were too stiff and cold to unbutton Glenn's

bearskin coat, so he left it on and followed Elliott to a table, trailing snow and ice behind him. Elliott brought him a mug of hot coffee and a plate of fish and chips. Magnus put a hand against his own cheek. He was so cold that he could feel neither his hand nor his cheek.

Several young men joined their table. Someone mentioned The Secret Bookstore. Then Elliott told them the two myths Matilda had shared with them at Glenn's deathbed. Magnus drank the coffee slowly as snow melted and dripped from his head and beard. His fingers ached as feeling returned to them. His eyes kept turning to watch Matilda playing. She never looked in the direction of their table, so Magnus didn't know if she had seen him enter or sit down.

When Elliott stopped speaking, one of the men commented on Matilda's beauty. Another man praised her talent at playing the fiddle. They both had business cards for The Secret Bookstore that they claimed Matilda had given them. Magnus looked at their clean-shaven faces. They wore new store-bought clothes, not at all like the homemade deerskin pants and bearskin coat he was wearing.

"I came as much to see her again, as to find the bookstore," one man confessed.

"You'd never know she was wealthy," another man said, pointing at Matilda. A gold watch glittered on his arm. "She'll inherit the entire forest when Amelia dies."

When he heard this, Magnus ached with sadness. He was

now poor and had neither a job nor a real home nor any special talents nor a purpose. He looked down at his bare wrist, remembering the Cartier watch he had left with Vincent.

Matilda was beautiful, and he looked unkempt. He was a coward, running away from Glenn's house to return to the city. He had nothing to offer her. The other men at the table were handsome, and he was sure that they would be much more appealing to a beautiful young woman. Magnus glanced at Matilda in the corner and then looked sadly down at the table in front of him, as he believed he now understood why Matilda had slipped away after Glenn's burial and never reappeared. She had no desire to see him again.

"It's comfortable here," the man with the gold watch said, leaning back in his chair, taking a drink of cider.

"Good place to wait out the winter," another man said.

"Is everyone here looking for The Secret Bookstore?" Magnus asked.

"Probably," the man with the gold watch said. "But right now we're enjoying life. Taking a break."

Magnus knew he couldn't stay here where it was warm and safe and comfortable. This would be an easy place to hibernate for the winter. But he sensed that many of these people would never leave here, even once spring came, feeling it was familiar and easier to remain. They had all been completely tamed. If he stayed here, he'd lose all momentum. He'd become as tame and docile and boring as these men at the table. He'd become somebody who would bore Matilda.

"I have to go," Magnus whispered to Elliott. "I need to go home."

"Where's that?"

Magnus shrugged, as he put on his winter hat. He didn't know.

Elliott whispered to the empty spot beside him and then looked at Magnus, his blue eyes wide.

"Robin says you'll see me again if you need me," Elliott promised.

"Say goodbye to Matilda for me," Magnus said, glancing once more at her fiddling in the corner, his heart tight in his chest. It seemed she had not noticed him come inside, and would not notice him leave.

Then to distract the wolves still guarding the way in and the way out, Magnus took his plate with the remaining fish and chips and set it on the floor at the doorway. The smallest wolf pounced at it. The largest one growled. The middle-sized wolf leapt in and lunged at the small wolf's throat. The large wolf bared its white teeth and leapt on top of the other two wolves. In an instant, the three wolves became a ball of grey fur and snapping teeth and snarls and yelps of pain and drops of flying blood. As a group of people gathered to deal with the fighting wolves, Magnus slipped out of the warm cabin to continue looking for the way home.

The Winter

Fatigue made Magnus' arms and legs feel like wood. He thought he would just rest for a moment against an oak tree. But once he sat down, he was paralyzed by exhaustion and fear. He wept, and the tears formed icicles on his cheeks and froze in his beard. The snow fell non-stop for several days, until layer upon layer covered him.

Magnus sat there all winter.

His mind became quiet.

More snow fell.

Magnus saw love in the space between snowflakes.

The shadows of birds moved across the ground, tied by invisible strings to the birds themselves. In that gap between the shadow and the birds, love dwelt.

Several stubborn oak leaves that had continued to cling to the tree finally fell. They twirled through the air and landed around Magnus. The shadows of the falling leaves were as real as the leaves. At the same time, the shadows of the falling leaves were as temporal. In their own time, both would disappear as they met the earth.

The sun set before him each evening. On clear nights the moonlight cast the shadows of tangled tree branches and trunks across the blue snow. These shadows looked like a new type of hieroglyphic language—the silent voices of the trees hovering over him, casting ethereal nets around him.

Once, several lynx stopped and stared at him, as though trying to determine if he were alive. Two of the young lynx teasingly nipped at each other. They play-fought, becoming a rolling ball of fur on the snow before him.

A coyote approached, and the lynx scattered. As the coyote neared Magnus, it flattened its over-sized ears against its head, bent down, and nudged the snow away from his hand. When Magnus did not move, it nudged his hand harder. Magnus remained immobile and it walked away, swishing his face with its scraggly tail.

A squirrel scampered across a branch of the oak tree above him. A clump of snow fell on Magnus' head. The squirrel leapt to a nearby tree and disappeared.

One day at dusk six deer, two large bucks and four does, stopped beside him. The last female neared Magnus. She twitched an ear. One of the bucks flared a nostril. The others remained motionless. Minutes passed. The buck craned his neck to look around. The does dug in the snow with their hooves until they found and ate the acorns that had been deeply buried beneath the snow. Suddenly, one of them stopped chewing and looked directly at Magnus with large soft eyes. She leapt into the air and sprinted away. The other deer bolted behind her.

Ravens flew to the top of a snow drift in front of Magnus. They sat and slid down and stopped at his feet. Then they flew to the top of the drift and slid down all over again. They seemed to be enjoying the ride, like children, and trying to tempt him to do the same.

Once, at a great distance, a shadow that resembled the form of a human glided by. It did not pause to study him.

All these things impressed themselves on Magnus without him needing to comment or evaluate or judge them. Poems poured into him as if whispered into his heart. He remained frozen and unable to write them down. But he felt no need to do so. Just hearing the words was enough.

He forgot why he was in the forest, sitting alone against a tree.

Early in the winter, he cried several times because of the beauty of it all. Later on he shed no tears, for he felt neither sadness nor joy. He was at peace with all that moved around him.

He knew winter was the promise of spring. The forest needed scarcity to make room for the gluttony of the coming new growth. To be filled up with poetry, he needed to be just as empty and silent.

The Moonlit Chase

One March day, Magnus heard distant cries that sounded like children calling out to each other. Several dozen swans flew westward. After several minutes, the flock changed direction and flew back the way they had just come from, as though they had all impulsively changed their minds, still honking loudly to each other. Then three or four split from the group and flew north. A solitary swan flew south. After several more minutes, they all flew in different directions. It seemed that all that mattered was that they soared through the sky simultaneously.

Beneath Magnus, the earth creaked as it shifted and adjusted with the rising temperature. He broke the ice off of his index finger and wriggled it. He did the same to a second finger and then an entire hand and arm, flexing his limbs as he went. He twitched his eyebrows, nose and lips, so snow fell from his face. With great effort, he stood, and the remaining chunks of snow and ice fell and shattered on the ground.

His hair reached his shoulders and his beard touched his

chest. His shoulder blades jutted out through his skin, and he could feel his ribs poking through his shirt. He walked slowly through the forest, regaining strength in his legs with each step.

He felt so peaceful with his decision to remain in the forest that it did not even feel like a decision. Instead it was like an answer had risen in him through the winter.

Magnus instinctively knew he should head straight east to find Glenn's house. This ability too seemed to have developed by listening to the silence throughout the winter.

On the way he found a tiny bird's nest made of fine grass, fallen out of a tree, onto a melting mound of snow. He wrote in his journal:

Survival

I could live
in this tree

in this nest
in a tree
that does not break

when it falls

At Glenn's house, he sat at the kitchen table for three days and nights, writing poetry.

Then he stopped to eat and sleep.

After he woke, Magnus went out to look for The Secret Bookstore. He found and followed coyote tracks, deciding it would be easier to track the animal than randomly searching the forest for the bookstore. He searched for prints, scat and markings. As he tracked the coyote, he felt no loneliness. Instead he felt a connection to the animal he was tracking, the trees and the memory of Glenn, Elliott and Matilda, like they were all hovering around him.

At dusk he came upon a tree that had been recently cut down. A note was pinned to the trunk. As with the other notes, this one claimed the woodcutter was searching for The Secret Bookstore. After Magnus read the note, he sniffed the air. The smell of skunk competed with the fresh scent of sawdust. When he searched the area for the trespasser's footprints, he found a skunk snuffling under some bushes.

Magnus leapt away and scrambled up the first tree he saw, a large maple with thick branches. He climbed as high as he could and perched on a limb. The skunk glanced casually up at him, as if Magnus was a dull and insignificant curiosity. Although the skunk hadn't sprayed, a dank odour still hung around it. Not wanting to surprise or anger the creature, and provoke it into spraying, Magnus sat motionless, wrinkling his nose, breathing through his mouth, to avoid the stench. The skunk lowered its head and ambled a few feet away, where it began to dig in the earth with its sharp front paws. It dug up and ate some grubs and then meandered farther away.

In the dim evening light Magnus continued to sit in the tree, waiting to make sure that the skunk was gone. A few moments later, he was startled by the sound of branches snapping and breaking on the forest floor. A man carrying an axe on his shoulder, and mumbling to himself, emerged from the brush. Magnus' heart pounded, as he realized that this was the trespasser who had been cutting down trees.

"Stop! Trespasser!" Magnus shouted.

When the woodcutter looked up and saw Magnus, he dropped the axe, turned and ran away. Noticing that the man limped, Magnus thought it would be easy to catch him. Magnus scrambled down the tree, cutting his right cheek on a branch on the way. Only as he thudded to the ground from the tree and a sharp pain pierced through his knee did he remember his own limp.

The man ran on without answering Magnus' shouts to stop. Magnus followed close behind him. In the light of the full moon he could clearly see the shape of the man and the dark outlines of tree trunks and branches.

They crashed through the trees and underbrush for hours, alternatively running or walking or hobbling. Several times they both paused to catch their breath. Then Magnus would lean over and rub his throbbing knee. Each time, the other man made the same gesture.

After a few moments either Magnus or the man would start

moving and the chase would continue. At times, Magnus was so near the trespasser that he could smell the man's sweat. They were both too breathless to speak.

Finally, Magnus stopped. His knee screamed with pain, and he was too exhausted to go farther. The man stopped too, panting heavily. Magnus grabbed him by the arm, even though he doubted that he'd be able to restrain him, for he was so tired. The man weakly pulled his arm away from Magnus. Then he threw a feeble punch at Magnus' jaw. Magnus turned in time, so the fist just skimmed his face. Both of them threw punches at each other, most of them glancing off their targets.

The interloper took a few steps away from him. Magnus followed, but tripped over a tree root. As he stumbled forward, he fell against a large rock. He groaned as excruciating pain sliced through his knee. Magnus took a deep breath to steady himself. He noticed the air was heavy and putrid. Various white rocks of different sizes glowed in the moonlight, and Magnus realized that they were in the lowland of the book cemetery. Nearby, the trespasser sat still and dropped his head to his chest. He clutched his right knee with both hands.

"I give up," the trespasser said gruffly, breathing heavily. "We're at the book graveyard. Might as well surrender. I buried my life story right here. It's dead and done. Truly, a poorly lived life it was."

He raised his head to look directly at Magnus. Magnus was shocked to be staring at a person who looked exactly like himself.

Shadow-Side

In the bright moonlight, Magnus could see that the other man wore clothes identical to his own. He was the exact same height. His hair was also long, and his beard scruffy. He too had a cut on his right cheek, just under his eye.

"I didn't think I'd ever be caught," the man said. "And never by you. What are you going to do with me?"

"Who are you?" Magnus asked, confused. "Are you from the past, or the future?"

"Neither. I'm your shadow-side." The trespasser stood up. He moved slowly, almost languidly, stretching out his left leg and then his right.

Magnus' heart pounded loudly in shock, as his skin turned cold and clammy and his knee screamed out in pain. He stood up, trembling, realizing that he was not looking at a possibility of himself, but a part of himself that he had not known existed.

He inched backwards.

The trespasser stepped towards him.

Now that they had both stopped breathing so heavily, Magnus noticed the singing of the spring peeper frogs. While tracking during the day, he had found the sound peaceful, but standing there with the trespasser, the sound seemed ominous. The moaning of one tree branch rubbing against another, made him shake even more.

"Why did you cut down all those trees?" Magnus asked. He thrust his hands into his pockets, and clenched them into fists.

"Would anyone just give a man like me a book?" the trespasser snapped.

"What's wrong with you?" Magnus asked. "Why wouldn't the bookstore owner give you a book?"

"You know why. I'm not good. I'm a coward. I'm weak. I'm lazy. I'm stupid. I'm unworthy." As the trespasser spoke his lips curled in a sneer. He seemed unafraid to confess these things. In fact, his confession sounded more like an accusation.

"Are there qualifications for receiving a book?" Magnus pulled his hands out of his pockets and kept them in fists at his side, as he wondered why he was standing there arguing with himself. The icy fingers of the night air were sharp against his sweaty skin, and he shivered.

"If there aren't, there should be," the trespasser said, stepping closer to Magnus. "I knew I didn't qualify, so I thought, what if I came all this way and didn't receive a book? I had to steal one."

"Of course."

Magnus nodded, understanding. For although he wanted to convince the trespasser that if he had found the bookstore, he would have received the book he wanted and needed, as he paused to consider his next words in the argument, Magnus realized that he didn't believe it himself. His shoulders slumped, for he knew the trespasser's thoughts had been his own. He had successfully suppressed them before they had fully formed.

When he saw the recognition on Magnus' face, the trespasser smirked and said: "Disturbing, isn't it? Your shadow will always be connected to you. Either you will see it rising up to meet you, or trailing behind. You'll never escape me."

Magnus knew that he had to take the trespasser to Amelia, as Glenn had told him to when he found the man cutting down the trees. He did not worry about forcing the trespasser to come, for he realized he could not get rid of him, now that he had caught him. He could never outrun someone who stuck as close to him as a real shadow.

"Do you know how many trees I cut down? How many trees you destroyed?" the trespasser jeered as they walked together through the dark forest.

"It wasn't me. You did that. I'm not taking responsibility for what you did," Magnus stated firmly.

"But you didn't stop me, did you? You didn't want to stop me because you're as greedy and cowardly as I am." The trespasser snickered.

Magnus was silent.

In response, his shadow also stopped speaking.

Magnus' shoulders tensed. His mind buzzed with wild thoughts that tussled and fought with each other, so that none of them made sense.

The Secret Bookstore's Owner

Pale pink morning sunlight trickled through the trees, as Magnus and his shadow-side entered the clearing in front of Amelia's home.

Magnus glanced back at the trespasser, who walked right behind him, close as a shadow. Magnus stopped still. The man bumped into him. As they stared at each other, Magnus saw him more clearly now that there was thin daylight. Twigs were caught in his hair and beard. His bloodshot eyes were wide above sharp cheek bones that were prominent in his thin face. Dried blood crusted the cut under his right eye. He stank of sweat. Magnus cringed, realizing he looked and smelt like this man he loathed.

Amelia and Matilda both stood, waiting, at the farther edge of the clearing, past Amelia's house, near the river. Matilda wore the same green dress as she had the first time Magnus had met her. His joy at seeing her was tempered by his embarrassment of being seen with the dark shadowy man at his heels, and his fear of how he must look to her.

Amelia had wrapped a green and brown shawl over her layers of skirts, dresses and shirts. The raven sat on her shoulder and cawed loudly, uneasily ruffling its wings and swivelling its head from Magnus to the trespasser.

"Who is this?" Amelia asked, pointing at the trespasser with a bony finger.

"He's the man who has been cutting down the trees," Magnus quickly responded, relieved that Amelia realized that the other man was the interloper.

Amelia shrugged her shoulders and the raven flew up into a tree. The trespasser rubbed his face and blood oozed from the cut. Magnus touched his own cheek and looked at the bright red blood on his fingertips. He wiped his fingers on his pants.

"Give him a book from The Secret Bookstore," Amelia said.

"You're the owner now," Matilda said.

"Me? The owner?" Magnus stuttered.

He felt dizzy and stumbled backwards, until he touched an oak tree behind him. He leaned against it, and it felt like the tree was leaning against him in response, holding him upright. With his back against the tree, he felt less faint.

"Of course, you're the new owner," Amelia said, removing her shawl with a flourish and draping it over her arm. A wisp of her white hair fluttered as she did so.

"You inherited it from Glenn, and with it the job of giving

the books away," Matilda said, standing on tiptoe and then falling back to the heels of her feet.

It was like a fog lifted from Magnus' mind, and a great weight rose off of his chest. Magnus instantly recognized what he had been missing all this time: the awareness that The Secret Bookstore always had been there in Glenn's home. He stepped away from the tree and immediately felt dizzy again. He inched backwards and again pressed his back against the firm oak trunk. Again he felt better. He simultaneously felt a mix of confusion, joy and relief.

The people he had given books to had been able to see and understand what he had not. Why hadn't Glenn told him? What had prevented him from seeing the truth?

"You didn't know? Fool," the trespasser mocked in a low gruff voice, and laughed.

Another jolt of awareness shot through Magnus as he suddenly recognized the trespasser's voice as the one that he'd been hearing since the car accident. A sharp pain pierced through his knee, and Magnus clutched the tree behind him with both hands. The shadowy figure that he'd kept seeing from the corner of his eye, disappearing before he could have a full look, was this sneering man before him.

Magnus sank to the ground, and sat against the oak tree.

"It's impossible to see truth through fear," Matilda said, kneeling beside him. "That's why you didn't understand before."

She took Magnus' hand in her own, and tugged his arm, until he slowly stood up. She continued to hold his hand in her own small, warm one.

"Magnus, you've done a perfect job of giving the right book to the right person, even when you didn't know you were The Secret Bookstore's custodian," Matilda said.

"Come," Amelia said. "We'll go there now, and you'll pick out a book for this trespasser."

"But that would be rewarding him for destroying trees," Magnus protested, shocked. He had expected—no, he wanted— some harsh punishment for the trespasser: jail or a large fine or hard labour chopping wood or cleaning out bird cages.

"The books you give are not a reward," Matilda said.

"Pick the one he needs," Amelia added. "Simply do what you have done for everyone else. That's your only job. When Glenn was here, he gave away many, many books. Now it's your turn as the new owner of The Secret Bookstore."

"I don't understand," Magnus said, rubbing his cheeks.

"Soon enough it will all be clear," said Matilda, rising on her tiptoes and then rocking back on her feet. "Trust us?"

Magnus hesitated, and then nodded.

Choosing A Book

Once they reached Glenn's house, Magnus went to the wooden throne outside his bedroom window to choose the right book for the trespasser. A plump mouse sat on the stump. Magnus expected the mouse to move, but as he bent over it, it remained immobile and stared at him. He picked the rodent up and set it gently on the ground. It darted to the corner of the house and sat under a fern, and watched him.

Magnus took his place on the stump and closed his eyes. He visualized a vulture circling overhead, until his mind was quiet. Then he looked deeply into the trespasser's heart. He saw darkness. The trespasser would never be satisfied; for when he had one book, he would want more, and he would be afraid of losing the one he had. Magnus understood this, for when he loved someone, he automatically feared losing them, as he had with Matilda.

He looked even deeper into the trespasser's heart. In a flash, he saw many letters of the alphabet that floated into words and then sentences. There were endless lines of unwritten poetry. Fear had prevented his shadow from ever writing down a poem. The multitude of the trespasser's unwritten thoughts weighed him down, making him far too heavy to walk on water.

The trespasser had never drawn animals towards him. He had never seen the beauty of this forest, for his fear kept him focused on his doubtful thoughts. The trespasser did not know Glenn or Elliott because he refused to be guided by anyone or anything, except his own fear. The trespasser wanted to know the secret of how to walk on water, but he would try to sell the book Magnus gave him, or sell the secrets.

As Magnus looked into the trespasser, he stopped fearing him, and the trespasser was powerless over him.

Now Magnus felt pity for the trespasser. He was hardly more than a child who had been taunted and teased and kicked and tormented, and believed everything that anyone had ever said to him or about him. As he moved towards compassion, Magnus' inner eye visualized a light on his leather book, which contained the notes and poems he had written throughout his journey. He kept his eyes closed for several more minutes, hoping the light would move to one of the books on the shelves, for he didn't want to give away this one.

He opened his eyes. The mouse still sat under the fern, watching him with its beady black eyes. Amelia and Matilda sat under several pine trees, with the trespasser between them.

Magnus let his shoulders relax, only then realizing that they had been hunched up around his ears. The peeper frogs sounded friendly again. Even the pain in his knee eased a little.

"Ready?" Amelia asked, almost smiling. "We'll bring him to the edge of the forest and send him on his way with the book."

The raven cawed and it seemed to Magnus the sound was friendly, encouraging.

Matilda gestured with a slender hand towards the house.

Magnus nodded at the women. He went inside, retrieved his journal from the bookshelf and brought it out to them. The trespasser's face lit up when he saw it, though his eyes remained furtive. He tried to snatch the book, but Magnus jerked back.

"You can have it at the forest's edge," he said sternly.

The trespasser snarled at him, but Magnus' fingers tightened on the journal.

"Come. Let's go," Amelia said. The layers of her skirts fluttered as she walked away from them. Matilda followed close beside her. For the briefest moment, Magnus thought he saw both of the women's feet rise above the ground.

The Disappearance

As they walked to the edge of the forest, Magnus continued to clutch his journal. The raven flew ahead from tree to tree, and every few minutes rested on a branch, waiting for them to catch up. The air was cool, except where dappled sunlight filtered through the trees and reached the forest floor. At these patches, Magnus slowed and paused, wanting to feel the soft warmth on his face, for the sunlight felt comforting and strengthening.

At one point the raven disappeared. It returned a few minutes later and dropped something shiny and silver onto the path. The trespasser darted ahead and snatched it up, waving the item high above his head in triumph. Magnus recognized his Cartier watch as the trespasser fastened it onto his wrist.

"I don't need it," Magnus said. "You keep it. That time of my life is past."

Magnus smiled inside, thinking that the pun sounded like something Glenn would have said.

Within fifteen minutes, Amelia led them to a place where the forest opened into a field, near a stand of poplar trees. Magnus marvelled at how easy this journey was in contrast to how he had struggled to find his way in the snowstorm last November.

"Give the trespasser the book," Amelia told Magnus. "Let him go."

At first, in response, Magnus instinctively clutched his leather book even more tightly. Then he forced himself to loosen his fingers, and he reluctantly passed the journal to his shadow-side. Magnus' heart clenched. The trespasser snatched the book and quickly glanced through it, as the Cartier watch on his arm glinted in the sunlight. Perched on a low branch, near their heads, the raven ruffled its feathers and cawed.

"You'll miss me," the trespasser told Magnus.

The raven cawed again. The trespasser turned his back on Magnus and strode out of the forest. Magnus' knee screamed in pain as the trespasser walked away, and he fell to his knees, unable to stand upright.

With each step, the trespasser faded into less than a shadow, until he was just a translucent image.

"What's happening to him?" Magnus whispered.

"When you bring the dark into the light, it cannot survive," Matilda said softly. "The light overwhelms it."

The trespasser completely disappeared. Magnus' watch vanished with him, but the journal dropped to the ground. The raven cawed a third time.

Magnus looked down at his own hands, and then back at the place where the trespasser had stood. His shadow had disappeared, but he, Magnus, was still here. Goosebumps covered his flesh.

For the first time in his life, he neither longed for something nor desired to escape something. His world—his life—was full of possibilities. He felt light and young. His knee had stopped aching. He stood up, and raised his leg and swung it backwards and forwards, marveling at being able to move it easily without pain.

Magnus bent down and took off his hiking shoes and socks. He walked barefoot across the ground to the clearing, stepping carefully to avoid sharp sticks. He picked up the journal and paused, as a soft, warm breeze lifted the hair from his brow and rattled the new spring leaves of the poplars. Every sound around him—birds, his own breathing, and the whisper of dry leaves under his feet— echoed the peace inside of him.

The movement of a single turkey vulture circling overhead also echoed his peace. The vulture flew in descending circles. Magnus sensed that it was coming near to acknowledge him. It came so close that Magnus heard the rush of its flapping wings. When it was at the tree tops, it rose and flew up towards the sun, until it became a speck in the sky above.

He opened his journal and wrote:

Resurrection

I receive
a new heart

of flesh

I stitch it to my sleeve

it beats regularly
rhythmically
religiously

I feel foreign
to myself

yet
I am
more myself
as I am removed
from my

self

The Postman And The Map

Magnus returned to where Matilda and Amelia waited in the forest.

After several steps, Magnus caught sight of something in his peripheral vision. About twenty paces away sat a postman in a rocking chair under a pine tree. He wore the same blue uniform that he had when Magnus had first met him with Glenn just outside the city the previous fall. Beside him was the same porcupine. He was again petting it, wearing the same leather gloves, as the porcupine gnawed at one of the legs of the rocking chair. The postman rose and waved, when he saw Magnus, Matilda and Amelia.

"Any mail for me?" Magnus called out, feeling hopeful, expectant. "I'm Magnus Fox. I live at The Secret Bookstore."

"Magnus Fox. Let me have a look!" the postman exclaimed, in a jovial voice.

Magnus approached him, still bare-foot, carrying his shoes by their laces around his neck. Matilda and Amelia followed.

They stopped a few feet from the postman and the porcupine. The animal stopped gnawing the leg of the chair, clattered its quills, and glared at them.

"He still doesn't like strangers," the postman said, as he stood and opened the large cloth sack on the ground beside him. Reaching in, he took out a handful of letters and glanced through several. He paused and looked up at Magnus with a wide grin.

"Here's a letter addressed to you. Fortunate you came by. Very fortunate," the postman said, handing the envelope to Magnus. He happily slapped his knee with his postman's cap.

Magnus took the mail. His name was handwritten on the front of the envelope. Below his name in the same handwriting he read: *The Secret Bookstore.* There was no return address. He opened it and removed a piece of yellow paper that had been folded several times into a thick square. After he unfolded it, he saw it was a map. He spread it on the ground and knelt to look at it.

On the paper was a hand-drawn map of the forest. Glenn's and Amelia's homes were sketched and neatly labeled. A river ran in front of Amelia's house and several dozen enormous ancient trees stood across the river. One of these large ancient trees had tiny, precise writing on its trunk that said: *The Secret Bookstore.* A small wooden door at the bottom of it was carved with the image of a dragon.

An arrow pointed from this tree to a corner of the map,

where someone had drawn the inside of the tree trunk. The curved walls were lined with shelves holding thousands of books. A tiny figure stood at the bottom holding a candle, casting light around him. The man had a long beard that rested on his chest and long hair that touched his shoulders. Magnus recognized himself in the figure.

As he closed his eyes, Magnus remembered the future. He visualized himself entering the tree, looking up in awe at the books. He sniffed, knowing the air in the tree would be heavy with the scent of musty paper. He understood that these were all his books to give away to those who sought the store.

"Extraordinary," Magnus said, as he pictured everything happening as he spoke. "I have to walk across the river, open the door of the tree, and go inside. Then I'll give away a book to each person brave enough to give up his life for a poem I have written in the back of it."

As he realized all this, Magnus felt his soul expanding until it seemed to encompass the entire forest. As he kept giving away books, he knew his soul would grow larger and larger. To be filled up with love and peace, he had to continually empty himself of the poems he heard inside of him. To be filled with poetry, he had to fill himself with silence.

He had become so absorbed in the map that Magnus had forgotten Matilda's presence. He suddenly wondered in panic if she had slipped away, like at the waterfront and after Glenn's burial. He opened his eyes.

She was still there. He sighed in relief.

"You're not leaving?" Magnus asked Matilda.

"Where would I go?" she asked, standing on tiptoe and then rocking back on her heels.

"Will you stay here with me?" he said. "I have a good reason that you need to remain with me."

"What's that?"

"I love you."

Matilda smiled. Magnus bent towards her, and they kissed.

On the return to Glenn's house, Magnus flew through the air, though his bare feet were on the ground. He kept looking at his feet, amazed that they were touching the earth with each step.

Matilda loved him.

He had never felt so light.

When Magnus tripped over a tree root and hit his knee against a rock, he hardly noticed the pain. Instead he joined Matilda and Amelia in laughing at himself. Their laughter bounced and echoed off the tree tops and trunks and resonated around them, until it seemed like the entire forest chuckled with them. Magnus was sure he heard the laughter of Elliott and Glenn joining in the echoes.

Looking at the pale moon in the morning sky, Magnus said:

Perspective

grow
        small

the distant moon
                                sees

there is
the entire
            world
gazing back

Living Life Inside A Story

On the way back to Glenn's house, they came upon the book graveyard. Magnus noticed that amongst the white stones, a green rock the size of his fist glittered in the morning sunlight. It was the same colour as Matilda's eyes and her glass bead necklaces. The ground in front of the rock was covered with yellow daffodils, red tulips and pink crocuses.

He saw a light dancing over the flowers, and Magnus knew there was a book buried there, and that it was meant for him. A gentle breeze touched his face, and a whispering sound passed by, and he felt suffused with love.

As the women watched and waited, he found a flat sharp-edged rock that he used to gently dig under the flowers. Not far beneath the surface, the rock clanged against something solid. He pulled out a metal box, and brushed away several clumps of dirt. The lid creaked as he opened it. Inside lay a book wrapped in a clear plastic bag. He pulled off the bag and read the cover: *The Secret Bookstore, by Magnus Fox.*

He opened the book to the beginning, and read aloud to Matilda and Amelia:

Once upon a September morning, Magnus Fox exited his condo and saw seven turkey vultures roosting on the shiny paint of his new red Porsche. Magnus shouted and dropped his briefcase. The birds slowly stood and shifted, as if they were in no hurry. He was so near he could see their short hooked beaks and bald heads. Waving his arms, he ran out into the parking lot.

"Will you read the ending?" he asked Matilda, passing the book to her.

Matilda flipped to the last page and read silently to herself. When she finished, she closed the book and handed it back to him.

"You don't need to read it. You're here already," she said.

"The ending is my beginning," Magnus said.

He nodded, understanding that he was right where he was supposed to be, and to be any other place would be impossible. "Truly, my story wrote itself in living. Life is lived inside of a story."

He wrote in his journal:

Walking Barefoot Through Life

the dark

paths of the past
are illuminated

by all
who have walked
across
            the river
                   before us

here the forest, hear
the stores of unending
stories

where the
       turkey
    vultures
circle

A single turkey vulture flew overhead. Studying the bird's gliding, Magnus understood that life was easier when he did not resist the winds. Life was easier still when he didn't fear the winds. Life was easiest of all when he loved the winds.

Matilda stretched out a hand to him, and said: "Ready?"

"Yes. I feel like Elliott today," Magnus said. "Just as young and fearless. Anything is possible."

Magnus and Matilda walked hand in hand towards the river.